While the
Messiah Tarries

While the
Messiah Tarries

STORIES

Melvin Jules Bukiet

HARCOURT BRACE & COMPANY

New York   San Diego   London

Grateful acknowledgment is made to *Antaeus*, where
"Gematria" first appeared, and *The Antioch Review*,
where "Old Words for New" first appeared.

Library of Congress Cataloging-in-Publication Data
Bukiet, Melvin Jules.
While the Messiah tarries: stories / Melvin Jules Bukiet.—1st ed.
    p.   cm.
Contents: Gematria—Landsmanshaft—The big metzia—The golden
calf and the red heifer—The Devil and the Dutchman—Old words
for new—Postscript for a dead language—Himmler's chickens—
The Library of Moloch.
ISBN 0-15-100083-2
I. Title.
PS3552.U398W48   1995
813'.54—dc20   94-38038

Designed by Lori J. McThomas
Printed in the United States of America
First edition
A B C D E

To Madelaine, Louisa, Miles

Contents

"I believe with perfect faith in the coming of the Messiah. Even though he may tarry, despite this I believe."

—MAIMONIDES,
Thirteen Principles, number 12
(recited by some European Jews entering the gas chambers)

Gematria

EIGHT EMERALDS lay on the pale green felt square. Rosensweig fingered the edge of the cloth. He had chosen it carefully to accent the color of the jewels. Had it been sapphires on display, he would have used his baby blue felt, and for rubies the delicate pink, but like everyone else on the block he had his specialty, emeralds, so that the bud-green cloth was used more frequently than all the others combined. For a truly colorless diamond, one that really incorporated the entire prism, he would have used the dead black cloth that sat underneath the rest, but he had never seen such a gem. Cynics claimed that utter flawlessness did not exist, but he kept the untouched cloth in his stack as a sign of faith in the idea of perfection.

The woman across the counter was a tall, sallow specimen, but Rosensweig had learned to refrain from judging people by their appearance. Besides, he was forbidden by religious strictures from peering too closely at the opposite sex. Instead, he tugged at his beard and allowed his imagination to roam.

The potential customer had come off the street and inquired at the counter in the ground-level arcade of the Gemstone Building about a special kind of emerald. They had directed her to Yitzy Nathan on the fourth floor. Nathan's stock, however, was blemished, and the lady had seen this at a glance. She waved away the loupe Nathan offered, and started out the door. Only by chasing her to the elevator had he been able to direct her further upstairs to Rosensweig, from whom he would expect a secondary commission if there was a sale.

The woman took the other end of the cloth from Rosensweig, as if they were newlyweds prohibited from touching for any but procreative purposes. With a sharp tug that emanated from the lady's braceletless wrist, she yanked the cloth out from under the emeralds and let it drop to the floor. She looked at the gems on the shabby blotter, and said, "Pallid."

"Fourteen carats."

"It is not the size I am interested in, but the quality."

Rosensweig nodded. "Please, wait a moment." He left the room, leaving the eight stones where they lay. Together, the cluster was worth as much as fifty thousand dollars, but Rosensweig did not worry. If one was budged, the alarm would be sounded, the exits sealed, and a private detective force surrounding the premises in minutes. There was no escape from the building unless a check cleared, or cash crossed the blotter. The only commodity Rosensweig valued as much as jewelry was cash.

It did not make a difference what nation had minted the coin. He was adept at rates of exchange and had dealt in pounds, francs, Krugerrands, and yen. He had once sold a brooch for a satchel full of Nigerian bearer bonds. These, too, had their own distinctive aura, like the gems.

He took the prize of his collection from his safe. It was a six-sided beauty loaned to him on consignment from a once-eminent banking family that had slowly been liquidating its assets. Per the

Tates' request, he had removed the distinctive antique setting in order to lessen the likelihood of identification, but a sophisticated eye could distinguish individual stones as easily as different paintings in an artist's oeuvre. Rosensweig himself could tell the work of certain Dutch cutters who had been dead for a hundred years. They were masters in the field, whose work was only appreciated by the likes of the elite on the penultimate floor in the Gemstone Building, the top floor itself reserved for the landlord.

The stone he laid down before the rude stranger was, to his mind, a real gem. He did not expect the sallow woman to purchase it, but Rosensweig wanted to put the intruder in her place. He wanted her to know that he was not just any huckster with a chip of fossilized carbon to hawk. He was Rosensweig, who had earned his place on the next-to-top floor of the precious gems mart that stood above the rest of the five- and six-story buildings on Forty-seventh Street, lofts and brownstones that had been converted into a labyrinth of interconnected cubicles like a flea market. He took a mirror from his vest pocket, breathed a rank gust of half-digested brisket and cherry soda onto the glass, rubbed it to a sheen on his tie, and set the mirror in the center of the blotter, the eight emeralds like so many pebbles beside it, and the Tate stone dead center.

The sallow woman brought her ringless pointing finger to her thumb and flicked the gem off the mirror like a marble. It clicked against one of the smaller emeralds and ricocheted to the floor.

Rosensweig dived after the gem. "How dare you?"

"I said that I want a stone with four sides, a natural square."

"Get out," Rosensweig shouted.

The lady tipped a dingy fedora.

"Besides, no such thing exists," Rosensweig berated her. "An artificial square can, of course, it can be constructed, but it is counterproductive. It is the interplay of light reflected by the facets that gives the gem its value. It would be to destroy the value. It would be desecrating the face."

The woman ignored him. She repeated her first request in a slow metronomic voice. "I want an emerald as flat as a mirror, as transparent as glass."

"Try a costume merchant," Rosensweig sneered.

"Thank you," the woman said and turned to leave. Her suit was unbuttoned, her necklaceless chest suggestive.

Rosensweig said, "You would have to pay a great deal for such a gem."

She glanced over her shoulder.

"Did I ask the price?"

"I will make inquiries."

"I will return on Tuesday."

ROSENSWEIG CLOSED early that day. He was about to take the subway back to his apartment, but he decided to stop to browse in The Erudite Angler, a bookstore harbored incongruously in the midst of the diamond district. For a secular institution, it maintained a remarkable collection of esoteric Jewish literature: a sixteenth-century Prague Bible, rare antique Haggadahs, manuscripts and documents, and, to Rosensweig's particular bent, mystical Apocrypha.

Every once in a while the dealer in commodities felt a compulsion to investigate the Zohar and other medieval texts that dealt in beauty and morality. He read stories of angels and wonder-working rabbis, and he dabbled in the Kabbalistic transliteration of names and numbers called gematria.

In Hebrew, letters serve as numbers too, *aleph* functioning not only as the English "A" but as 1, *bet* as both "B" and 2, *gimel* as 3, and so on through *tuf*, "T" or 400. Now if one takes the numerical value of a word or phrase and discovers another word whose value is the same, then one may assume that the words themselves are equal. According to gematria, the equivalence of numerical value revealed the secret truths evident beneath the surface of the language.

The proprietress was a disconcertingly pretty young girl who had inherited the store from her cantankerous father—a silver vendor until the day he gave up the noble trade in order to sell books on the street where all his friends worked. In addition to stocking dreck for the general public, the store specialized in works pertaining to jewels and Judaica. The owner recognized Rosensweig, and said, "Sir. We have just received a letter from Gershom Scholem to Walter Benjamin qualifying the nature of quiddity. Perhaps you are interested."

He averted her eye, but he nodded. He was interested in anything to take his mind off his disturbing visitor.

The girl smiled at the man's modesty, and led him up a narrow side staircase, his eyes glued to the worn rubber treads on the steps lest he inadvertently catch a glimpse of stocking. Unfortunately, the rare book room upstairs was occupied. Caldos and Freund were there, engaged in a heated discussion that they did not deign to interrupt on his behalf.

The attic space acted as an informal club for those merchants like himself who were interested in more than money. Of course most of them had not reached the financially rewarding position on the eleventh floor of the Gemstone Building that Rosensweig had, but he usually enjoyed their company. Today, however, he wished merely to contemplate matters that he knew in his belly intimated more than they acknowledged.

Caldos finally raised his head and saw Rosensweig and smiled. Caldos was an Argentinian Jew who had smuggled a pasha's ransom out of Buenos Aires in a whip handle that he ostentatiously clutched through customs, and converted into a horde of the most obscene gold-plated nonsense north of Times Square. He specialized in works of crude anatomical explicitness and sold them to the commuters who traversed the block twice daily on their path to and from Grand Central Station. As the commuters' glazed eyes passed over the finer goods of better men, they were gripped by the shocking vulgarity of Caldos's merchandise. The gaucho winked and hinted that their tawdry innuendo would persuade women to indulge in acts of untold licentiousness. "Monkey see. Monkey do," he leered and sold the gimcracks as fast as the trashmakers of Hong Kong could produce them. Later he transferred his profits back into the rarest of species. He bought from Rosensweig and the rest of the eleventh-floor elite after extended negotiating sessions over the loupe.

"What are you saving for?" the native-born Jew asked him once.

"Exile," Caldos replied, disdaining the country he lived in as he pandered to its worst impulses, and prepared his cache so that he could leave on a moment's notice, bullwhip once more in hand. "No place else is safe, and anyone who thinks it is is merely deluding themselves. America in 1990 is Germany in 1930 is Spain in 1480."

That was what Caldos and Freund were arguing about. The former said, "For a Jew, the only home is the Galut, the Diaspora. The natural condition of the Jew is exile. That is why I cannot be a Zionist."

"Every Jew must be a Zionist," Freund retorted.

"So that is why you live in Brooklyn?"

Freund, a mild and taciturn Dutchman, had arrived in New York twenty years before as a representative of the Amsterdam bourse. He had originally been frightened by Manhattan, but grew quite comfortable when he discovered that Forty-seventh Street was of the scale and mentality of a small village in the midst of the metropolis. He snorted, "I help sustain the Israeli economy more than any Sabra. I am there on business three times a year. Just next week."

"Always next week. Always last week. Never this week. You are here every day, Freund. Who are you kidding?"

For once, Freund could retaliate with perfect effect. He opened his brown jacket and removed a packet with plane tickets. He waved them and laughed.

Caldos turned to Rosensweig, and asked, "Are you here for our appointment?"

"No, that is at your office, on Friday. I am here because of a different appointment." He told the two men about his curious visitor.

"A flat emerald. Bah, she doesn't know anything," Caldos scoffed.

Freund, as always, was more reflective. "But what an idea. Where did she get it?"

"Gentlemen, I am sorry to break up this chat, but in case you haven't noticed, the store is closing, and I am sure that you have wives waiting with broiled chickens." It was the proprietress of the shop, her disembodied head speaking above the worn wooden spindles at the landing.

"Ah, chiquita," Caldos sighed, although, like his more reverent peers, he too did not dare to meet her glittering green eyes. "If I had such as you to greet me, I would be like Freund here, never leave home."

Freund slapped at his head, but missed.

The girl stepped generously aside to let the men leave without the risk of touching a female. She understood their customs and their laws.

ST. VALENTINE'S Day had just passed. It was a big season for Caldos, and he was flush with cash. He had made an appointment with Rosensweig for another purchase, nothing so grand as the Tate stone, but one or two of the bright green octet perhaps. Carrying the merchandise in a leather bag strapped to his waist, Rosensweig arrived to find the door to Caldos's emporium ajar. There were a hundred figurines on the shelf performing a hundred acrobatic variations of the same basic act, like the façade of an Indian temple. Caldos was still sitting in his chair, his whip wrapped about his neck three times, his face as blue as a sapphire.

Rosensweig reached to call the police when he noticed a message scrawled on the pad beside the telephone. It said, "Keep the Corner."

"The corner of what?" Rosensweig wondered, and he felt the same chill he first felt when he held one of the Tate emeralds, which rumor had it had been cut from a single natural square. He was certain that the strange visitor's inquiry the week before had set the tragedy in motion, and that her return visit would provide the explanation. He decided to let the police discover the crime by themselves. He could not help Caldos. If, however, he could do something to assuage the pain of the man's immortal soul by waiting, he could do it best without the interference of secular authorities.

"What else should I do?" he argued with himself. "Tell them to watch for a killer with a penchant for Kabbalistic imagery?" Even the men who gathered in the rare book room would not believe him.

THE TWO weeks between murders was the worst period in Rosensweig's life. The sallow-faced woman never returned to inquire about the gem, and in the meanwhile he was suspicious of everyone on the street—the other men like himself in their earlocks and dark gabardines; the fleet black teenagers who served as runners between buildings; the hot-dog sellers, both kosher and non; and even the hired policemen who patrolled the block on behalf of the merchants' association, but could not protect it from such insidious evil. There was no telling who the maniac was. Everyone was a candidate. Rosensweig refused to enter an elevator with another person for fear that would be Caldos's assassin. He hired cars to drive him home, and then abandoned the cars halfway across the Williamsburg Bridge for fear the driver was the killer. Then he walked back across the bridge against the traffic to make sure there was no car following him.

The Pierre Menard Tower in which Rosensweig lived alone was the tallest building on the Lower East Side. It was built in the 1920s to cater to those from the immigrant sink who had prospered, but did not want to move out of the neighborhood to the Grand Concourse in the distant Bronx. It was a luxury building in a slum, complete with a Babylonian frieze that circled the elegant lobby. Unfortunately, the building was finished the week before the stock market crash. The leases that had been signed were broken, and Mr. Menard leaped off the roof of the vacant structure that had been his dream.

When he arrived home, Rosensweig perused his usual correspondence which included a trade publication sent from Jerusalem. An item at the bottom of the front page caught his eye. A visiting businessman, Freund, had been stabbed thirty times, his pockets emptied except for a ruby the color of blood. The report was ironic, the criminal considered stupid, having stolen a tourist's nonnegotiable American Express checks while ignoring a valuable gem. But anyone who ever worked on Forty-seventh Street knew that Freund never dealt in rubies. He was strictly a semiprecious man.

He was stabbed with an antique letter opener from the Tate Collection. A phrase that was not released to the press was allegedly found scrawled on his forehead in blood. Rosensweig felt that he could see that wide furrowed expanse, and the lettering that read, "Keep the Corner."

SINCE THE sallow-faced woman still did not call Rosensweig, and it was her safety he worried for more than his own, Rosensweig went to the police. He explained his intuition to a desk sergeant, who was barely polite enough to refrain from laughing at his uncommon informant.

It was infuriating. Rosensweig practically cried, "Don't you understand? The third killing is only a matter of time."

"I understand that you are distressed at the murder of your friend, and how well did you know Mr. Caldos, sir?"

The man was impressed that Rosensweig knew the unreleased message, but assumed it was Talmudic deduction or street gossip. Nothing was confidential here. These men had been self-dealing for millennia, and no local law could erase the bond between them.

Rosensweig told him about Freund.

"We do all that we can, sir, but the murder of an American national on Israeli soil is not our domain."

"Well, it is mine," Rosensweig fumed and stamped out to the street.

The first thing he did was to call upon Yitzy Nathan on the fourth floor of the Gemstone Building and ask him, "That lady, the one you sent to me. What did she look like?"

"I don't know."

"You must know."

"And what about yourself?"

Rosensweig could not say that although he was too pious to peek at a lady's face, he assumed that Nathan was not. He tried another tack. "Did she ask you for a flat emerald?"

"*Ach*, it's nonsense."

"The customer is always—"

"The customer is always an idiot."

"But can you do it?"

"Of course, I can, but I won't without the entire price as down-payment. Otherwise, I can take it and flush it." He made a crude sound.

Rosensweig took a roll of bills from his pocket.

But Nathan still wouldn't admit that he had looked at the woman.

The next day, however, Nathan called Rosensweig on the telephone, and told him to come quickly.

"I'll be downstairs in ten minutes."

"No, not here. Meet me in the rink at Rockefeller Center."

The spot Nathan had chosen was only around the corner, but it was another world, a public realm, a Christian realm, one in which he presumably felt safer than on the block the Jews called their own. There was the collection of gigantic office buildings, and at their base there was the famous gilded statue of Prometheus, beneath whose benign glow the skaters circled. They were a picturesque bunch, mufflers flying, and the girls in skirts shorter than shameful.

Rosensweig approached the rink just as Nathan clutched his chest. At first people assumed that he was struck down by a heart attack at the sight of such lewd women. Of course, no one heard the shots in the midtown clamor, but the blood spread and stained the surface.

Rosensweig ran forward and took a parcel wrapped in brown paper and rough twine from Nathan before the first skaters came to a halt in a succession of glittering sprays of ice.

Nathan was shot by six diamond bullets, although the police had to drain the rink in order to separate the most lethal of the missiles from the ice in which it was embedded after passing through his vital organs. They strained eight hundred gallons through a sieve until they caught the diamond, along with seventy-nine cents in change dropped by the skaters. A pearl-handled revolver was found in the garbage with the words *Rosensweig expected* scratched upon its barrel. The gun was from the Tate Collection.

DESPERATE, ROSENSWEIG had no choice but to return to the police. Once more, he never got past the desk sergeant. Before he could say, "Rockefeller Center," the man knew what he was there for. "The third corner, correct?"

"And you're going to wait for the square."

"You're crazy."

"People are dying."

"It happens everyday."

"Not in this manner."

The sergeant asked him, "You ever hear the joke about the grandfather who asks his grandson 'What's red, hangs on the wall, and whistles?'"

"'What?' asks the grandson.

"'A herring,' he says.

"'But Grandfather,' the boy complains, 'a herring doesn't hang on the wall.'

"'You can't take a hammer, and wham, nail a herring to a wall?'

"The boy thinks about this and then says, 'But Grandfather, a herring isn't red.'

"'What, you can't take a paintbrush, slap slap some red paint on a smoked fish?'

"'Yes, but Grandfather, a herring doesn't whistle.'

"The grandfather looks the boy straight in the eye, and says, 'So!'"

Rosensweig stood back in horror. It was the very idea of motive-lessness that shocked him. No, he refused to believe the implications of the sergeant's story. This was not random, but he could not offer the literal-minded policeman an answer to his unspoken question. He thought of his gematria. There was a sense to the atrocity if only he could discern it. There was something that bound a ruby, a sapphire, and a diamond murder, and perhaps it was something that only an emerald murder could complete. It was something that bound the cities of Amsterdam, Buenos Aires, and Jerusalem, that he could not yet grasp. They were points on a deathly compass.

The crestfallen merchant retreated to his office, where he ran the numbers and letters backward and forward until he was dizzy, and then the telephone rang. It seemed to wake him from a trance. He was surprised to notice that it was dark outside. The telephone rang again. He looked at it as if it was a rhinestone, and picked it up. Nobody did business after hours. The street was empty. "Hello," he said.

"It's Tuesday."

Rosensweig looked out his window of three-quarter-inch glass, covered with wire mesh and steel grate, lined with a mercury alarm, eleven floors over Manhattan and a sheer drop to the street. He discerned meaning in the configuration of the office towers that loomed on either side of the block lost in time. He discerned meaning in the pattern of pedestrians crossing Fifth Avenue against the changing of the lights, from emerald to ruby. For a moment in the split between the change, he thought he saw a diamond-colored third eye, but in the blink of his own rheumy eye it disappeared. He discerned meaning everywhere but his own realm of numbers, names, geography, and gems.

He thought he was alone in the building except for the guard on duty downstairs, but the guard did not buzz him to tell him that he had a visitor. Yet he heard footsteps and he thought he recognized the slow deliberate tread, although he could not recall where he had heard it before.

Rosensweig jumped to his feet and dashed out to the hall in which he heard the familiar steps, but the hall was empty, and the door that led to the staircase to the penthouse was open. That was

where the office of the company that owned the building was lo-
cated. Rosensweig had mailed his rent there every month for his
twelve years as a tenant, but he had never been upstairs.

Apparently the penthouse was smaller than the other floors, a
single room with a desk and two chairs and some office machines.
The only decoration on the wall was a city tax map with the com-
ponent lots of the block outlined in faint red and blue ink. The
Gemstone Building was outlined in green.

He heard additional footsteps behind a pair of sliding-glass doors
which opened onto a terrace where a dark silhouetted figure waited
for him. From a distance, he could tell that it was a woman, and
suddenly he knew who she was. The last time he had heard her
steps, he had followed them above the bookstore. If the proprietress
of The Erudite Angler had disguised herself as the sallow woman,
she had done so to no necessary effect because he hadn't dared to
look into her green eyes, which would have been to violate the
principles of his culture. Nevertheless, he stepped out onto the
terrace.

She welcomed him, "The scholars of the middle ages, men like
yourself with all the time in the world, believed that they could
determine the future of the world by ascertaining the mystical significance of numbers."

Gematria. "They also believed in Shabbetai Zevi. The false
Messiah."

"*If* he was false."

"He drove them into an eschatological panic. They gave away
everything they owned and abandoned their homes, because they
had been told that they would not need material possessions at the
end of days. And then what did he do? He converted to Islam. He
ruined them."

"Perhaps Zevi's prophecy was implicit in his apostasy. Perhaps
his message was that Jews ought to intermingle with the peoples of

the earth. They must bring the exile to an end. They must embrace the Galut."

"Galut," he said, and began to spell the word in Hebrew: "*Gimel*, three wraps of the cord like tefillin; *lamed*, thirty stabs of the knife, *vov*, six bullets in the gun, *tuf*, four hundred. Four hundred what for me?"

"It's an address. Four Hundred Fifth Avenue."

Rosensweig knew the neighborhood as well as any jewel in his inventory. "It doesn't exist."

"Not yet."

"I don't understand."

"*Tuf* is also the last letter, the one that completes the alphabet."

"I know that, but I cannot make the recombination. I still do not understand why you brought me here."

"Because I am tired of living in exile. I want the emerald, Rosensweig."

"I do not have it. It does not exist."

"It exists and you are standing on it."

He could not help but look down, but all he saw was the rough surface of the roof. Was there a secret compartment? Allegedly the building was riddled with them. He scuffed at the asphalt.

"Beneath the floor, and eleven pathetic floors in the city that scrapes the sky, Rosensweig, keep digging until you hit the greatest jewel on earth. A green square, Rosensweig."

"I still do not understand."

"Gematria, Rosensweig."

He began to spell the word, "*Gimel, mem . . .*"

"The hell with Hebrew. The bunch of you are so isolated, you can't imagine that there is any other language beside the Bible's. Take the language of the Galut. Caldos could see that. That was why he looked me in the eye."

"And Freund and Nathan?"

"I killed them to get to you, Rosensweig, to acquire the square emerald, fee simple."

"But—"

"The Tate emerald, Rosensweig. Realign the letters. Call it an anagram if you wish. They spell Real Estate."

He played with the letters in his head. "An 'M' and a 'D' are missing."

She answered in the overly inflected mock-Yiddish tone of a policeman, "So?"

So the Tate emeralds were a fraud, a sham. In a world pregnant with reference and depth, her heart's desire was literally, physically, as shallow as a God could make it. It was the surface of a surface, the counterfeit of a counterfeit, falsehood squared. Only a woman could conceive of such a diabolical craving. "Land," he sighed.

"Yes," she said. "A plot of land, right here on Manhattan Island. That's the jewel."

"And your father ran a bookstore."

"And before that he sold silverware, dinner services for four, for Godsake. But he couldn't afford the rent, and he went out of business—and what business did he go into? Books, because in those days the real estate was cheap. But he was stuck in the idea of the Galut. Books and jewels, transportable wealth, transportable wisdom. Yet he owned the building that damn store was in, and now I own this one."

"Land," Rosensweig sighed.

"I own half the block and have options on the other half. The only problem is that most of you bozos have twenty-year leases, and you may be willing to wait for the Messiah, but I am not. I want you out and running. Then I can demolish this whole lousy warren, put up a building of Cor-ten steel. A perfect black diamond."

"But why me?"

"Because you're influential, a leader of the community, a pillar of the eleventh floor. If Rosensweig breaks his lease they will all go, because they know that there is no way he will forgo the benefit of his below-market rental unless he is convinced of some supernatural evil. When you start running so will everyone else."

"I'm not convinced."

"If you won't run, Rosensweig, you'll fly." She approached him, a woman, untouchable. He backed up to the edge of the roof and thrust out to her the only offering he had managed to acquire, the pane of deep green that he had taken from the corpse of the man whose death defined the third corner. "Nathan made this."

"Die, Rosensweig. There's no place in today's world for you." And she pushed him, and he fell to earth, or pavement, precisely where the canopy with the number 400 that was represented by the last letter of the Hebrew alphabet would hang.

So what if an "M" and a "D" were missing. Maybe she would rent to doctors. At least their learning was not mystical, but practical. There was always a message to be found in language. She learned that in the bookstore.

She looked at the green square Rosensweig had brought with him. It was glass. She ground the lure underfoot, bent, and blew away the dust.

Landsmanshaft

PINCUS KICKED at the mound of dirt in the New Utria Cemetery. Freshly turned and orange in color, the heavy clods stuck to the underside of his orthopedic loafer as he bid Alexander farewell. The last time he had spoken to the newly deceased was thirty years before. The last words he had said to him were, "I'll dance on your grave."

Pincus looked sheepishly at the rest of the crowd, who knew of the long-standing animosity between the two men—if not the lethal vow. There was Poller and Teitler and old Boiberik, who cackled incoherently while his Jamaican nurse tried to drag her octogenarian charge away from the edge of the perilous dimple in the ground. There was Rabbi Beckenstein chanting a prayer and the deceased's only son's only son running a finger inside his collar to ease the chafing on his neck from the tie he rarely ever wore as he listened to the description of the grandfather he never knew.

Many of the mourners were related, but so distantly they could not trace the link. No matter, they were more than merely friends or third cousins; they were landsmen.

Whether a born Knihyniczean currently resided in Jerusalem or

Rio or Rego Park, his first loyalty was to the patch of Eastern Europe, this year Poland, next year Russia, where his ancestors had encamped five hundred years before. Of course, the Jews knew that such lodgings were always temporary, but they had gotten used to Knihynicze, and fifty years after fleeing, they still missed the sound of the Easter bells calling their neighbors to the massacre.

Pincus tapped his foot to loosen the remaining clump of earth, and wondered if that counted as a dance in the divine reckoning, or if he must outrage them all to fulfill his oath, throw his hands up to the sky, as if the occasion was a Hasidic wedding, and stamp on the developing mound.

It had been a long trip from Knihynicze, whose graveyard—a sprawl of wooden markers that trailed off into the fields of sugar beets—the mourners all remembered with greater or lesser fidelity, to this city of stone. The New Utria Cemetery was so vast that it had its own internal road system and a jitney to shuttle mourners to the various quadrants of the necropolis. In the face of such morbid grandeur, even Manhattan rising in the distance resembled a row of gigantic granite tombstones.

Weiss whispered to his brother, "Cemeteries are the best business in the world."

"Why?"

"You buy by the acre and sell by the foot."

Between the memories of one cemetery and the actuality of the other, those who gathered to pay their respects to Alexander had all lived out the vision of Emma Lazarus. Brought across the ocean by the magic words, "freedom" and "opportunity," they experienced a tenement existence of poverty, prostitution, and the grim humor that bubbled like a life-giving spring in the urban Sahara.

By the time Alexander took up his penultimate residence in the Beth Israel intensive care ward, he had known more of both comedy and tragedy than most men of his generation, yet his last thoughts were not of the plush aisle seats in which he spent his professional life, but a warped wooden pier overhanging the gray Baltic Sea. That was where he last saw his own parents, who promised to meet him "later."

"Life is a lie," he gasped to the intern, who closed his eyes.

Alexander arrived in New York as a pale, frightened adolescent with an envelope containing his uncle's address on Rivington Street and the polite request to take in this stranger from across the ocean, a request which was refused.

"Never mind," he said, and got a job sweeping the floors at the *Forward*, Abraham Cahan's Yiddish tissue that held the daily more diverse population together with muckraking tales of urban scandals, personal ads placed by *zaftig* widows and their unmarried daughters, stories by Singer, and poetry by Grade. Unknown to the management, their new copyboy slept in the shadow of the presses, until, self-taught, the time came for him to step to the other side of the typewriter, and find himself a byline instead of a home.

Alexander's theater reviews made him a celebrity. One typical column began, "A new drama called *Cleaning House* opened at the Lyceum last night, but if cleanliness is next to godliness, this should play in the ninth circle of Hell." He was viciously unsentimental and knew that everybody turned to his column even before the personals.

In the intellectual stewpot of East Broadway, there was much psychologizing about the denizens, and the assumption in the cafeterias was that if Alexander's relatives had been any more welcoming, he would not have been so spiteful later in life. But while he was pitiless toward the failures of the stage, he was generous to those few less fortunate than himself who met the same difficulties as he did in the land of opportunity.

Luckily, none of his landsmen came within the scope of Alexander's professional opinion, so he was never compelled to foul the nest from which he emerged. Neither playwrights nor actors, most of the Knihyniczeans were tailors and cobblers and other garment-industry drudges. The more enterprising owned their own shops. A few scribes painstakingly hand-lettered Torahs for the hundred-odd synagogues in the area, but the closest to Alexander in proximity if not character was Pincus, a typesetter at the *Forward* with philosophical interests. Although Pincus's fingers were always dirty, Alexander, a dandy, never disdained the proletarian. The two men enjoyed each other's company, and Alexander often gave Pincus theater tickets Alexander could not use. Pincus courted his wife-to-be on Alexander's leftovers.

Pincus thought back to a large cafeteria on the Lower East Side. Outside, lines of clothing hung over the streets like yachting flags, while from the gutters pushcarts sold screwdrivers and galoshes, as they circled around the barrels of brine that contained sour, half-sour, and dill pickles, which were protected by heavy wooden lids from contamination by the chicken feathers that flew through the window of the slaughterhouse on Essex Street. Other vendors cried to the women behind the fire escapes to sharpen their scissors, or to the men to buy holy books nearly as ragged as their would-be readers.

Inside the cafeteria, the steam from the trays of meat and boiled fish condensed on the curved glass counter underneath a mural in which allegorical figures standing for agriculture and industry joined hands above the body of a tophatted banker lying prone in a bed of dollars.

"It's Lehman," Alexander said.

"No," Pincus disagreed. "Guggenheim."

"No," Alexander insisted. "Lehman or Loeb or one of those families with the killer children."

"Who can tell the rich apart anyway," Pincus laughed. "They have no character."

Alas, the cafeteria closed when the newly enfranchised descendants of the original settlers abandoned the neighborhood and Lebetkin could no longer make the rent on the sale of iced coffee to the codgers who remained. Before the site was demolished, however—to make way for a Chinese day-care center—the mural was carted off to the Jewish Museum, subsidized by the rich whom the blintz-eaters detested.

"Hmph," Alexander snorted. "Life is a museum."

More vividly, Pincus recalled another afternoon when the revolutionary mural still rang a red chord in the souls of the diners, and Lebetkin's pastrami dripped with the juices of life, and the trees on the boulevard were a coppery orange speckled with a white dust that blew from the marble cutter, who was the only tenant, for the great arched vault under the Williamsburg Bridge.

Alexander was wearing a double-breasted suit with padded shoulders that made him look like a gladiator. They were talking about the cemetery plot owned by the community association, 100 by 100 feet deeded out of the middle of the New Utrian territory, surrounded by a cast-iron picket fence. Between bites of his herring-tomato sandwich, he said, "Sell that shabby turf."

"Never."

"It's the only asset the landsmanshaft has."

"It's the only tie to the past the landsmanshaft has."

"Sell it to some of these white-bread yids." He gestured out onto East Broadway to the American-born Jews he disdained nearly as much as he envied them.

The friends met frequently at the cafeteria, and the question they argued most vehemently was really one of forward thought, one man advocating a bold stride into the future while the other clutched ahold of the past.

"All I'm saying is that the association has better things to do with its cash."

"Like what?"

"Invest it so that we can have a little something to spend while we can still appreciate it. Buy everyone a new pair of shoes. Throw a party. Put on a play—hah! Life is a play."

"And what about when you die?" Pincus was always the morbid one.

"Scatter my ashes on East Broadway."

"Then you know what will happen on Simchas Torah?" This was the holiday when the congregation left the synagogue to celebrate the giving of the law in a wild Hebrew conga line.

"What?"

"I'll dance on your grave."

To which Alexander, the man of modernity, free of the superstitions of the Old Country, turned white, clutched his heart beneath a checkered ascot and cried, "A curse. You put a curse on me."

Of course, Pincus had not intended any such thing, but his pride would not allow him to recant. It was the kind of argument that could occur a million times without effect, but, given just the wrong interpretation could also poison a friendship forever. Pincus regretted his haste, but Alexander's arrogance would tolerate no less than a fully abasing apology. Pincus looked around nervously, hoping that there would be someone nearby to make light of the incident, or somebody like Michigan the landlord in opposition to whom they could unite.

But the only witness to the episode was the man behind the counter, who was carrying a large tray of fish in from the kitchen to replenish the supply, his tense forearm revealing the tattoo of a Polish eagle. He stopped and watched the two erstwhile friends standing across the mica-flecked linoleum under the two muscular men of paint, as if modeling the primitive allegory.

"Did you see that?"

The man smiled. He had listened to the Jews arguing for years, copies of the latest *Forward* rolled up, brandished as if to train re-calcitrant puppies. They argued politics, and language, and Zion-ism, and money and children, and sometimes they came to blows. Come to think of it, there was very little that would not cause a ruckus here.

"A! How can you say A, you schmuck? B!"

"What do you mean, B? Any idiot knows A. My grandfather knew A before he drew breath. B, hah!"

"Hey, Velvel, what do you say? Tell this schmuck B."

"B?"

"You see, ignoramus. Velvel says A."

"A?"

"So, nu, if not B and not A, what, then?"

"C."

But this was different. There was something in the very silence that was more potent than all of the verbal attacks.

"Tell him, Jesus," Pincus implored. He was begging the counter-man for the right joke to save the day before an ill-advised comment over a perennial issue wrecked the friendship that had traversed the sea.

But Jesus was the most unpredictable member of their commu-nity. He too had come from Knihynicze, but he was not Jewish. Yet, his family had lived in the village even longer than the Jews. His father was, in fact, the Lord of Knihynicze, and that was how his son got his nickname.

Another Christian might have been offended, but Jesus rather enjoyed the irony, and encouraged it. The more savage his behavior, trapping and torturing small animals, and bullying the local Jewish children, the more pleased he was by the name that evoked mercy. He retained it when he came to America after a gambling scandal led him to theft, disgrace, and disinheritance. A foreigner for the first time in his life, he strode up the cast-iron steps of the Hebrew Immigrant Aid Society to demand a place in the community of those he had scorned.

A special meeting had to be called at the offices of the landsmanshaft to determine how to deal with the intruder. "The bylaws say that anyone born in Knihynicze is entitled to our help."

"Bylaws, schmilaws. The spirit of the law will be violated by a *momzer* like that."

"He's not Jewish."

"It doesn't make a difference if he's Jewish. He's not decent."

"It doesn't make a difference if he's decent, as long as he's from Knihynicze."

In the midst of the din, Pincus muttered to Alexander, "Do they really have to argue?"

Alexander said, "Life is a debate."

Pincus shrugged, "I suppose it's good for the lungs."

And the debate continued. They stood on chairs and screamed and shouted, and finally a basic charitable influence won out. Lebetkin offered the newcomer a job until he could find a more comfortable arrangement in a Polish neighborhood.

That had been years before, but the man was a hard worker, despite the malevolent eye he still cast over his clientele.

Jesus said, "Some more baked haddock, sir?"

Alexander, who now realized that the curse had been witnessed by this man, which made it twice as awful, stormed out of the cafeteria.

———

"YOU'RE WAITING for him to say a few last words perhaps?"

Pincus was jolted from his reverie. He was holding the shovel with which the last remaining population from Knihynicze was going to cover the late, unlamented Alexander, assisted in their symbolic labors by the professional diggers who waited to be summoned in the shade afforded by a large tombstone marked "Lebetkin and Lupowitz."

"Wasn't that a deli?" Poller muttered.

Sure enough, the engraving under the names read, "Two to go."

Teitler said, "You gotta have a sense of humor to spend your life with your arms up to your elbows in pastrami brine."

"You mean your wife has to have a sense of humor."

"You mean she has to have no sense."

"At least no sense of smell."

The men standing in a cluster behind the current wielder of the shovel exchanged comments. All the mourners were wearing dark suits, now that Alexander was gone. The critic had made a point of wearing red at funerals. If not a full suit, he wore a red tie or red suspenders. "Life is a costume party," he had said once while he and Pincus were still on speaking terms. "Why should death be any different?"

Pincus wondered if Alexander was buried in his red suspenders.

Off in the distance, one of the diggers unwrapped a bologna sandwich and took a can of beer from a bright plastic cooler. The sleek aluminum surface was beaded with condensation. The digger rolled the can across his forehead and sighed as if he had just taken a gulp.

The diggers had excavated the trench, and lowered the coffin on heavy canvas straps. An ingenious mechanism allowed the straps to slide out from under the coffin. At New Utria, death was a science. They had loaded a quantity of dirt equal to the volume of the coffin onto a truck to be carted away and sold for fill. Because the cemetery was Jewish, the replacement of the remaining dirt atop the clean pine box was left to the mourners.

Michigan, the landlord, was first, thrusting the shovel vigorously into the mound and tossing great sprays of dirt through the air, as if working on the foundation for a new building, until someone tapped him on the shoulder.

"Not too much space left."

Pincus looked around at the dwindling few souls who traced their ancestry back to the shtetl thirty kilometers southeast of Lublin. "Not too much needed."

"Perhaps we can sublet the extra?" Michigan mused, as he passed the shovel.

"On a monthly basis."

"The tenants in your buildings wouldn't know the difference."

"What are you inferring?"

Slotkin, the teacher, corrected the man of the world as he reluctantly tipped a token crescent of dirt onto the coffin. "The word is imply."

"What?"

"You imply; I infer."

"So what are you inferring?"

"Nothing," he said, eyes raised as a sign of innocence as he passed the shovel to Teitler.

"Didn't Alexander live in one of your buildings?"

"Briefly. He was always late with the rent, so I threw him out."

"You took a landsman to court?"

"Court, bah!" Michigan spat to the side. "In those days, a tenant didn't pay, you told the super to set his things out on the street."

"Didn't they get stolen?"

"Nah. In those days people had respect for the individual." He spat again, retrieved the shovel from Teitler, and threw a few more heaps of dirt onto the nearly obscured casket.

SO ALEXANDER stood on the sidewalk, manila folders full of his clippings beside him. There was no furniture, but there were plenty of clothes, from ties to tails to tallisim. Life was an opening night.

Pincus stopped by and said, "Looks like a scene from Chekhov."

"This never could have happened in Russia. Say Clifford Odets."

"You mean you go to the legitimate theater, too?"

"The legitimate theater," Alexander repeated, tugging at his goatee. "Does that mean ours is illegitimate—the bastard child of Shakespeare by Molly Picon?" The critic was touchy. Any stray comment could provide the insult that broke the friendship, but Pincus ignored it in the face of the man's precarious situation.

"So where are you going with this dreck?"

"What did you call my worldly possessions?"

"Treasures. C'mon." Pincus helped the homeless Alexander up to his apartment, where he lingered for months, until the argument in Lebetkin's cafeteria, after which he moved out.

Fortunately, a young theatrical extra offered to let the eminent one share her sixth-floor walk-up with the bathroom in the kitchen. Of course, Pincus never saw Alexander's new lodgings, but he was told that the critic would take baths while the girl prepared Shabbos dinner.

When the chicken soup was nearly done, he would stand, proud of his dripping nakedness, to shake his goatee like a Schnauzer, and then complain that the boiling water would get his precious books damp.

This was the lady who bore his son. Three years later, she got her first break as the ingenue in a Yiddish production of *Born Yester-*

day. Alexander said, "It should have closed yesterday, but the best we can hope for is tomorrow," a self-fulfilling prophecy.

Every enmity is different. While Pincus endured his pain in silence, the young actress left her mentor behind in the apartment overlooking the slaughterhouse from which generations of chicken feathers flew every month. She and her infant son moved to the more receptive climate of Hollywood, where she proceeded to make a career raging against Alexander on the Johnny Carson show. "The thee-ayter," she sneered. "Let me tell you about the thee-ayter. There was a play on Second Avenue years ago and the leading man suddenly had a heart attack, so the stage manager announced this to the audience, and a little voice piped up from the back, 'Give him some chicken soup.' The stage manager said, 'Sir, you don't understand. The man is dead. Chicken soup can't help him.'—'*Nu*,' said the voice, 'it can't hurt.'"

After the laughter subsided, she looked into the camera and said, "Now let me tell you about the chicken soup in my life."

Alexander said, "Her life is a film. Mine isn't, but hers is."

THE RABBI was saying, "A man whose restless integrity drove him ever forward. . . . *Yisgadol, vayiskaddash, shemay raboh*."

The deceased's only descendant wept as he listened to the thunk of dirt on the cabin that would bear his grandfather to whatever future they were all destined. Finally he allowed himself to be steered from the hole in the ground by the rabbi.

Poller commented to Teitler, "He's great at brisses as well as funerals."

"Yeah, but nothing in between."

And the Knihyniczeans continued to pass the shovel. Some used the tool with a vigor belying the sadness of the effort, while others performed the same activity with a kind of tenderness.

One said, "You know, sometimes I think Alexander used a shovel too."

"Yeah?"

"For all the shit he slung. The man was not known for his delicacy."

"Did anyone say deli? What, you going out for a bite after?"

"Yeah, to Lebetkin and Lupowitz, they use a shovel for their pastrami."

Although the original owner was buried, serving now only as a table for the pair of lunching gravediggers, his son operated a restaurant in Midtown for a new crowd who paid better than this bunch. Pushing sixty himself, Lebetkin the Younger took the shovel and paused to say a few words, "Alexander always enjoyed a good brisket. He liked a pickle on the side. He never bothered anyone behind the counter. He was a real mensch, but—"

"But?"

Reluctant to speak ill of the dead, Lebetkin Junior nonetheless felt compelled to finish his sentence as if to add one more slice to a sandwich, "but he was a small tipper." Then he handed the shovel to the next man.

Michigan said, "If not for that family I would weigh twenty pounds less. May he live until the Messiah takes over his lease."

Weiss whispered to his brother, "You hear the one about the kid, his father tells him when the Messiah comes all the dead Jews will rise up, everyone will move to Israel. The kid says, 'But, Dad, Israel's a small country. Can't hardly fit the folks it's got now. If every Jew who ever lived goes there it will be a disaster.' Father looks at his son and says, 'Hey, God took care of Pharaoh in Egypt. He took care of Hamen and Hitler. Don't worry, he'll take care of the Messiah too.'"

The shovel passed.

"Old Boiberik, he can't hold up his putz to pee, how can he hold a shovel?"

"He saves his strength by having a nurse hold his putz."

"It must be healthy. He'll bury all of us."

The oldest man there, logical successor to Alexander, took a huge heap of dirt and let it drift off the edge of the blade like orange snow. Still clutching the shovel, Boiberik gave a eulogy with the inflected babble of an infant, only comprehensible to a parent.

"What did he say?" they asked the nurse.

"Life is a shovel," she said, and tugged the metaphor out of her charge's hands and passed it to Pincus, and for a moment all of them wondered about the extent of the typesetter's participation in the last rites of his ancient enemy.

The sun beat straight down so that the spiky fence surrounding the cemetery hardly cast a shadow, just a coal-gray bulging at the base, where a few weeds sprouted, the subject of endless contention between the landsmanshaft's legal committee and the New Utria corporation. Were the weeds the responsibility of the party whose land they germinated from or the party whose land they spread onto?

Alexander insisted on the "Yankee" solution to any question that involved the burial society. In the case of the weeds, he advocated letting them cover the fence until the New Utrians were sufficiently embarrassed to cut them. Unfortunately, the appearance of the cemetery mattered more to the Knihyniczeans, and Lebetkin paid for the weed removal out of pocket, although each time anyone who had a plot reserved in that pristine square entered his deli, he added a "death tax" to the pastrami.

MOST OF the stones were recent. A graph would show a steeply increasing population, followed by a gradual decline as the remainder tapered to insignificance. Nonetheless, they argued in a ridiculous contention for space.

"Where do you wanna be buried?"

"I dunno, someplace shady."

"Nah, then them bums come and sit on you all day, drink beer, leave orange peels behind, chocolate wrappers, who needs it?"

"Maybe, but it's hot."

"Not half so hot as where you belong."

"So maybe it'll be nice to see the living sweat a little."

THE LAST time Pincus tried to exchange words with Alexander was years after the debacle in the cafeteria. Rumor spread through the pressroom overlooking East Broadway that there was a phone call for Alexander from California.

After a thirty-second conversation Alexander walked past Pincus in a daze. Pincus realized that the phone call must have been serious, and was confirmed in his judgment when he saw that the usually impeccable knot of the critic's regimental tie was askew. He cringed when one of the less perceptive secretaries joked, "Can you get me an autograph for my autograph book?"

In response to the question, Alexander asked another question, "Why aren't there any Jewish alcoholics?"

"I don't know."

"And dull the pain?"

Alexander met Pincus's eyes. The critic said, "Life is a book. The ink is blood."

Alexander's son had died a particularly American death, and he was buried in the western state where his sports car had crashed into a ravine, his veins swollen with the vicious powders of the Orient. He left behind a son of his own by a young actress who resembled his mother.

And although most of the Knihyniczean seed did not lead lives of such dramatic disrepair, they were no less estranged from their parents than the late Alexander Junior. Just as these children no longer belonged to the community of Knihynicze when living, they did not return when dead. The generation of Alexander I was the dividing line. Their ancestors in Poland, their descendants in California, they were the human boundary, physically in the New World, emotionally in the Old.

PINCUS GIGGLED a little, sounding like Boiberik, and felt a strange weight in his hands.

"Wake up. Wake up." They shook the typesetter, dazed by the sun and the memories, holding the shovel poised. "What are you waiting for?"

"An apology, perhaps?"

A SHADOWY figure wearing an archaic caftan draped about his broad shoulders strode through the rusty gates of the Knihynicze landsmanshaft plot. His boots were made of musky animal hide and he seemed half animal himself, with a thick moustache and a silver pelt of chest hair visible between the metal buttons on his jacket. The buttons shone in the sun, and looked hot to the touch.

"Oh, Jesus," Pincus said.

"Sir," the man replied. "I heard there was a funeral, but I see that it's not you, Pincus."

"Not yet."

"When your time comes . . ."

Jesus was in a philosophical mood, but Pincus was not inclined to indulge him. He finished the intruder's sentence, "You will certainly know about it."

"In the meantime . . ."

"Yes."

"You are wondering why I am here."

"Yes."

"I came to see you dance."

YES, HE had remembered. It was too much to hope that the sole witness to the legendary quarrel would forget.

"The question this brings up," the man continued with a cheerful smile, "is which one of you will be here to dance on Pincus's grave?"

"I guess that I'll always have you."

"Yes," the man chewed on the corner of his moustache. On releasing it, one could see that the left side was stained with his digestive juices. "And what about me? Is there a place for me?"

"Where?"

"Here, sir. I am from Knihynicze as much as yourselves."

"But this is a Jewish cemetery."

"No, it is a dead person's cemetery. Everyone who is dead becomes a Jew. That's why so many Jews die, in haste to return to their homeland. That is why the forces of life detest Jews."

"We'd rather wait for heaven if you don't mind."

"I thought this is your heaven." He gestured to the army of tombstones, some larger than others, but none more lavish, because stone carving was not a Hebrew art. There were no angels, no madonnas, no floral tributes—just the phrases that linked the deceased to the community, "Beloved Wife and Mother," in visiting which the living set a pebble atop the monument to record their own memory, as enduring as stone.

Pincus couldn't help but imagine the stone that ought to rise over Alexander's grave, "Hated Husband, Absent Father, Cheapskate."

Then he wondered if the critic's flaws might be a consequence of the landsman's loss of the land. "Heaven," he repeated, and mused, "like Knihynicze?"

Jesus gestured expansively to the field of stone. "This is Knihynicze. They're the citizens. You're the ghosts."

In a way it was the same argument that split the two comrades in Lebetkin's, regarding whether a Jew ought to look forward or back. "No," he said quietly. "This is Knihynicze," he tapped the prayer book they had read from so reverently.

The Cossack reached forth and ripped out a page and wiped his mouth. "Gutenberg was no Jew."

"It is not a matter of mechanical reproduction. Before the book, even, is the word, the truth. Life," he said changing Alexander's words only slightly, "is a book. The ink is in the blood."

"What good did it do Alexander?"

It was a good question. Pincus looked down at the gentle mound that covered his long-time nemesis, the grave he had promised to dance on, and to the shock of the gathered clan he began to sway, first as in prayer, and then more rapidly, as at a wedding, the way his first macabre thought had it, but then in obedience to yet higher powers.

He began moving in the same erotic sway which lead to his birth, which echoed the dance of earth in space, and Jews on the planet, the infinitely sustaining repetition of jest and manner.

"What is this, a Jewish wake?"

He looked at the intruder from the past, and now Pincus smiled. But he was not dancing to avenge himself on Alexander. He was dancing as they had their entire lives, dancing in study, dancing in combat, so why not dance now, in death. "Life," Alexander would certainly have said, if he had been present in red spats to say it for himself, "is a dance." No, Pincus was not dancing on Alexander; he was dancing with Alexander, and, in whatever realm of the spirits he now inhabited, Alexander was undoubtedly dancing with Pincus.

The Big Metzia

METZIA AS defined by Leo Rosten:
1. a bargain
2. no bargain (used bitterly)

Originally meant something valuable that was found. The Baba Metzia is a tractate of the Talmud that deals with laws of possession and obligations of guardianship. It begins, "Two men are holding onto a garment."

IT WAS as if the streets were paved with gold—Gorky St. Kalinin St. Leninskaya.

Staggering amounts of money were available in the Soviet Union. Not only rubles, those laughable simulacrums of cash, but dollars, genuine George Washingtons. Millions of millions. Alan Lapidus, son and heir of the founder and president of Weslacks, was convinced that all one had to do was to travel eastward in order to reap one's share of the bounty. "It's the second largest economy in the world," Alan stated, "and they don't have rayon."

At least once a week he slapped some magazine down on his father's desk and said, "Look." The pages were filled with tales of deprivation and desire. He pointed to a photograph of a line of babushkas snaking down a wide Victorian stairway. The caption read, "Queueing for Shoes."

"Very nice."

Alan said, "It's the largest untapped market in the world. All we have to do is fulfill a tiny portion in order to dwarf Macy's annual net."

"So go," his father replied from behind the gray steel desk of his corner office that overlooked the double-parked trucks, dress-filled metal racks, and hot-dog carts of the garment district. "But I'm not putting up a penny."

Alan left muttering, "Money-grubbing bean counter."

Disdainful as he was, however, the son was as great a believer in the bottom line as the father. He found the purity of the concept of return on investment to be deeply satisfying. By judging one's peers and oneself on a rigid numerical basis, one always knew precisely where one stood. That was why it was so frustrating that he was unable to convince his father that there were profits to be made. Ever since Glasnost, he had smelled fortune beckoning. Unfortunately, he was not sure how to act on his basic intuition.

Alan started haunting Dubrow's, the vast cafeteria on Seventh Avenue where the last lingering socialist impulse that had created the garment unions decades ago played itself out on three allegorical murals representing the meeting of capital and labor above the steam trays filled with boiled chickens and haddock and mashed potatoes that came ready-made from cans the size of wine casks. Dubrow's was the large intestine of New York's garment-district gourmets. It was the only spot that could sell a ham sandwich and make it seem kosher.

Alan found the cavernous room echoing with shoptalk contemplative. Refilling a glass of Yiddish bubbly at the free seltzer table, he set aside the embossed folder from the conference he had not dared to tell his father he had paid two hundred dollars to attend, "Business Opportunities in the Soviet Union."

The busboy unloading a new tray of glasses to help slake the thirst of the district tapped the cover significantly and winked.

Alan looked at the busboy's pleats under his gravy-stained smock. The kid knew from fashion. On Dubrow's salary, he clearly had an eye for value. But the cut was unusual, so Alan reached out to knead the fabric between his thumb and forefinger with the kind of stark intimacy that would have earned him a morals conviction anyplace west of the Hudson. "Where did you get this?"

"Moscow."

That was when the neon lit over Alan's head. It didn't make a difference if he imported or exported. The press all said that the Soviets were willing to pay through the nose for the Made in America label, but in their ursine modesty the Russkies thought they had nothing to pay with. Alan's great revelation was that they were wrong: They had clothes of their own. He would arrange a straight barter agreement, with each side to pay for shipping its own goods.

Most of the stars of Seventh Avenue had originally come from Russia. Look at Calvin Klein, Ralph Lauren. Forget their new names, cut to the shape of society's order; how could they miss the opening of the greatest market of the century? A people deprived of American style for seventy years, starving for fashion, ready to trade. It was heaven.

Ivan, the busboy at Dubrow's, was an immigrant. He had arrived less than a year before, had bounced around from Brighton to the Bronx until he alit in the garment district. "Of course this position is only temporary," he said, and told Alan how he was trying to break into the heady world of transcontinental trade in his own small way, to organize a computer to send to his brother who still lived in Moscow.

"Perhaps I could bring it with me?"

"While you are there on other business?"

They clasped hands and shook until the man behind them said, "Excuse me, this example of international goodwill is most heartening to behold, but I'd like to get some seltzer."

Ivan and Alan were soul brothers who shared a single goal— call it cash, coin of the realm, loot, gelt, or the heavenly simoleon, it was all you needed to buy a prune Danish. Ivan had the knowhow, Alan the wherewithal. And so after a scant few additional meetings under the deco mural, the native invited the immigrant upstairs to utilize the Weslacks office and showroom.

The first thing Ivan did was to question the name of the firm displayed on a gigantic bronze plaque that angled across the glass-brick wall behind the receptionist's desk.

"It's short for Western Slacks. Jeans mostly. Informal wear. I tell you we could have been as big as Levi Strauss if not for . . ." he pointed to a photograph of the founder, his father.

"Weslacks," Ivan turned the name over. "Too bad you can't merge with Ex-Lax. Then you can be the only company to shit in your own pants."

It was an old joke. Alan ignored it and said, "Buzz us in, Julia." Before the receptionist could inform the elder Lapidus, he added, "Mr. Rogov is a salesman from California. Please forward any calls for him. This way, sir." Finally settled in his own private office that might have been mistaken for a broom closet if not for the vice-president's title on the door, he said, "So what's next."

Ivan put his shoes on the desk and reached for the telephone. "International operator, please."

Cables started arriving, and swatches from Vilna, and tongue and cole-slaw sandwiches ordered in from the corner deli between long-distance calls.

Julia, however, was loyal to the name that signed her paycheck. In less than an hour she put Alan's father wise to the hijinks taking place under his inflamed nostrils.

Mr. L. responded as anyone who knew him would have expected, like a maniac, "Forty minutes to Tashkent. What are you looking for, the ten lost tribes? Maybe your dead brother?" he ranted, making the ritual daily reference to a nine-year-old child who had died decades before, the very late sainted Robert, whose sneakers his younger sibling had yet to fill adequately. "And who's he?" Mr. L. stared at Ivan.

Before Alan could attempt to explain, the ex-busboy spoke for himself, "So this is the genius whose company is going to be the first to penetrate the iron curtain. I'd like to shake your hand, sir."

Despite the elder Lapidus's misgivings, he found himself drawn into the vortex of activity whose center was his son's new partner. Ivan hopped about the tiny cubicle engaged in brainstorming sessions in which ideas and speculation about foreign currency whipsawed back and forth like the yarn in a loom and shuttle. To his credit, Ivan warned both Alan and his father that until a deal was consummated, their figures were as bankable as a three-dollar bill. The only thing left was to make the trip.

"So go," the founder said to his son, "but be sure that you don't have any idea what you're going to do there. You've got to be flexible, spontaneous, irrational, idiotic." He built himself up a fine steam. It was his way of saying, "Yes."

"Thanks, Dad."

"Fools go to Russia where angels fear to tread." His father mangled the quotation, but was pleased with the reference.

Visas and tickets were obtained in a flurry of last-minute arrangements.

Julia opened a new file under "R."

IVAN HAD laid the groundwork well. Although he declined to return to the motherland himself, intimating a checkered past that might still offend certain elephant-memoried commissars, he packaged Alan together with Breitbart, a distributor of automotive parts whose business card read, "Trader of All Jacks." Together, they were not only able to command a better hotel rate, but respect from the government misled by its ex-citizen into believing that such a delegation represented the cream of Yankee commerce. Of course, Lapidus still had to pay an exorbitant fee to shepherd his partner's computer through customs, but it would have been petty for him to gripe.

Using the power of the American telephone, Ivan had arranged for a much-coveted black Volga sedan to idle at the visitors' disposal, as if to whisk no less than Beria off to some diplomatic powwow at the Kremlin. Recalling the humiliation of finding a cab on a rainy Manhattan Tuesday, Alan thought he could get used to this way of life.

From the moment the representatives of the textile mills of Novosibirsk clapped rough hands on his finely textured shoulder seams, the young Lapidus knew that he was where he wanted to be. While Breitbart ventured out to see the sights, Weslacks's v.p. ensconced himself in the lobby of the Cosmos Hotel, talking deals. Platters of smoked redfish were brought to him along with the rich Soviet beer that he considered importing as he grew giddy with the prospects for success. Alan sent off a telegram to his father, saying, "They're as smart as Jews, as industrious as Koreans, with the economy of Calcutta and the market of the United States."

Between Alan Lapidus and the sky, however, lay one obstacle, Igor Rogov, Ivan's brother, recipient of the famous computer, and translator. "At the service," he announced.

The first thing Alan noticed about Igor was that, like his brother, he wore a decent suit, a tobacco-brown houndstooth. The next day, however, Igor appeared in the same suit and again the following day. It seemed that scarcity, not quality, was the issue.

Although they appeared virtually identical, Igor was unlike his sibling in every trait. Where the new New Yorker was all wiry electricity, the Muscovite wore a perpetual hangdog look of discontent. Like Ivan, Igor was a tall, sallow young man, but his chin was shaded with the perpetual five o'clock shadow of post–Five Year Plan malaise, and his hair was lank and unwashed.

If Igor had been a driver, his manner would have been less important, and if he had been a funeral director, it might have been an asset, but as a translator his tone was in direct contradiction to his words. When Alan was euphoric, Igor was phlegmatic. No matter the American's raucous tales of life in the garment district, his hardnosed logic, or his maudlin saga of Weslacks long, hard climb to prominence, Igor delivered the various goods in the same dull drone.

Alan might have complained to Ivan in New York, but it was impossible to establish a telephone connection. He was on his own, and he had to solve the problem by himself. Responsibility was the flip side of freedom, as he frequently told his Soviet counterparts, gesturing as dramatically as Trotsky before the Kronstadt fleet.

Despite Igor's personal failings, Lapidus had gotten used to communicating through another voice. He liked it. It gave him time between sentences to formulate an oratorical phrase or a point of logic. He relished the weird formality that compelled him to comment upon national differences. He enjoyed his role as spokesman from another world, no matter the infelicities of the medium.

Besides, there had to be something to complain about, since everything else was so delightful. Far from the dingy necropolis of outdated nineteenth-century idealism, Moscow was a ferment. The hotel was filled with sweet young Moldavian whores who waited patiently while some cultural attaché from the KGB took Alan and Breitbart to the Bolshoi, where he enjoyed ballet for the first time in his life. It helped that the whores and the spies, as well as everyone else from waiters to ministers, were thrilled by the packs of Marlboros and souvenir cigarette lighters sporting the Weslacks logo that Alan handed out like John D. Rockefeller dispensing dimes to the needy.

Everyone in Moscow was an enthusiast, except when it came to their own nation, for which there was total contempt. Of course, all this anti-Communism came from the mouths of people who were on the party dole, but their hearts were in the right place—except for Igor Rogov.

Igor was the only one who didn't respond to Alan's American charm. He was the only one who saw through the hail-fellow-well-met routine. He was the only one who didn't heed the lectures on the American way of doing things and the magical market economy. For God's sake, he was the only one who didn't smoke Marlboros.

Breakfasting in the hotel dining room, Alan and Breitbart speculated that Igor was the last true Communist in the USSR, the only one disappointed at the taffetizing of the iron curtain, but they both knew that his sour manner was a matter of character rather than politics. Igor was a born mope, which wouldn't have bothered Alan in anyone but an interpreter. It was like being separated from one's own shadow.

Finally Alan grew so frustrated at Igor's obvious mistransmission of the sense of his dialogue that he interrupted a meeting in the Ministry of Trade to compel Igor to translate a joke, "Did you hear the one about this guy sent to prison, to Siberia say, and his first night there, lights out, he hears the other prisoners say, 'Sixteen. Forty-one. Ninety-two,' and with each number they laugh louder and louder. 'What is this?' he asks, and the guy in the bunk next to him explains that they've all been there so long, they know each other's jokes so well, that they've assigned a number to each joke. Fine. The next night, wanting to join the group when the lights go out, he shouts out, 'Forty-one.' Dead silence. 'What's the matter?' he wants to know. 'Yesterday everyone laughed.' His neighbor shakes his head sadly and says, 'It's the way you tell it.'"

Alan mimed throttling Igor, who repeated in his unchangeably dreary monotone, "'It's the way he tells it.'"

"Da. Da." The beefy Soviet bureaucrats understood.

"I love this city," Alan crowed and waited for the hollow echo.

Igor's dejection was contagious. It was bad enough during business hours, but Alan relished taking his would-be partners to discotheques, footing the bill with an American twenty, the black-market equivalent of four hundred rubles, or twice the average citizen's monthly salary. Yet Igor refused to drink and sat there like a priest at the Follies.

Nevertheless, negotiations were going well. After a few false starts, Alan had begun to climb the rungs of the Soviet textile hierarchy, meeting managers and district managers and central managers and ministers until he was convinced that he was dealing with men who could shake a hand. After one especially satisfying banquet that included the presentation of a videotape of a factory in Kiev that could not be viewed because no one had a videotape player, Alan decided that it was time to check out the retail sector, and said, "Igor, let's go shopping."

Despite the translator's stuttered objections, they grabbed the Volga sedan and set off from the protected confines of the hotel, driving past the U.S. Embassy, where thousands of people clustered daily to clamor for the precious few visas out of the land that the naive foreigner found so paradisal. They made their way through a tangle of nineteenth-century streets, toward Pushkin Square, where a line nearly as long as the line in front of the embassy waited patiently for McDonald's hamburgers, and they emerged on the city's main drag. Until recently it had been named Gorky Street, but in the rush to recant the Communist past it was renamed Tverskaya.

The moment Alan saw pants in the window on the road to Tver for six rubles, translated swiftly into thirty cents, list, he knew that he did not even need to barter for his inventory; to purchase was sufficient. "How can I get, say, ten thousand?"

The translator who possessed only one suit looked at the American as if he was a madman. Ten thousand pairs of pants, worn one a day and summarily discarded, would last for thirty years.

"Not for me . . . for business. . . . To sell, Igor. To make money."

At the continued expression of bafflement on the face of the young man who had supposedly been representing him, Alan wondered how one brother could be so savvy while the other was so straight. He finished the businessman's catechism and then threw his hands up in frustration, "What have we been doing for the last week?"

"I do not know."

"It was a rhetorical question."

"I don't understand 'rhetorical'?"

Alan said, "Okay, Mr. Practicality, let's find someplace to sit down, have a cup of coffee. I'm going to give you a lesson in basic economics."

Of course there was no coffee to be found, but they sat down anyway, at an overpriced tourist café. At the bottom of a cup of ochre liquid, a light seemed to come to the student as it had months before to his teacher. "Would you like some ties?"

"To tell you the truth, Weslacks specializes in pants, but if you've got some ties, yeah, I'll look at them."

"Here," he extended the trapezoidal tongue of the tie he was wearing. It was the color of mud. "Pure silk."

Alan reached out in the swift touch of appraisal. "Not bad," he declared. "How many? How much? Those are the vital questions. How many? How much?"

For the first time, the interpreter was not at a loss. He answered immediately, "Two hundred thousand for five cents American each. Ten thousand dollars."

"I can multiply," Alan said. "How can you get—two hundred thousand you said—for a nickel each?"

"It is simple for the correct person. I know that you are saying that you are climbing up to the top, but here you must climb down to the bottom, to the one who has his fingers on the merchandise, because he is the one who ultimately controls it."

"Sticky fingers, heh?"

Igor frowned. "We do not have much detergent, it is true, but the Soviets are a very clean people."

"Let's just say that I'll take the ties."

For the first time a smile came to Igor's doughy face.

Alan could imagine his father's expression when he got the news. Nevertheless, it was Alan, not his father, who was the representative of his nation, his faith, and Weslacks in the Soviet Union. Once he committed to purchase the ties, his word was his bond. He wired to New York and sent the money to his emissary's account at the Vnesheconombnk.

Their last night in Moscow, Alan and Brietbart threw a party in the hotel lounge for their various friends. Nearly a hundred people sat at a single long table underneath a bright, unfaded rectangle on the wall where a portrait of Stalin may once have presided over all gatherings. The spirit of Stalin remained and there were several uneasy jokes about microphones under the table.

"Yes, in the lumps of bubble gum," Alan said, wondering how far the technology of such devices had advanced.

Then the factory manager who had it in mind to waylay several weeks' produce for his own personal gain, stood up and gave a toast to the foreign visitors. After he was finished, everyone at the table turned in Alan's direction.

Igor whispered, "They expect you to speak."

Made expansive by several tumblers full of herring-flavored vodka, Alan had no problem with such an impromptu performance. "First, I wish to thank the brave and generous Soviet people for opening the gates between our two nations. Too long have they been closed." He went on for a few minutes paraphrasing Robert Frost, and then he got down to particulars. "The first person to thank is a man whom I have never had the good fortune to meet, but is certainly present tonight in spirit if not flesh. Without him, none of us would be here. I refer of course to the man behind Glasnost, Prime Minister Mikhail Gorbachev."

There was a low murmur from the Soviets who were not as enamored of their former leader as Lapidus was. They responded more effusively when Alan began to name the people around the table. "I especially wish to thank Mr. Moisevitch, Mr. Kaspar, and Mr. Nechayev from the Union of Textile Manufacturers, and the generous folks from Cotemnicki."

He proceeded to work his way around the table, pausing for Igor to catch up with him every five names or so, until they came full circle to, "And of course, my traveling companion, Breitbart." By now, Alan's head was woozy with the flames of the vodka he had raised to his lips whenever one of the dignitaries had saluted him in kind. "You know, I nearly brought my wife along, but Breitbart's more fun—just kidding, everyone. I guess that takes care of everyone. Oh, how could I forget, last but not least, Igor, my invaluable translator, without whom nothing I have said tonight would have been understandable," he slurred.

Waiting for Igor's familiar echo to praise itself, it struck Alan that invaluable should mean the opposite of valuable, and then he said, "I hope that you will all come to the United States as soon as possible."

There was a round of applause, but the speaker could not relinquish his position. He continued, "In concluding, I will repeat the statement a great American president, Andrew Jackson, made when confronted with the possible dissolution of the early republic."

Where did he get this stuff from, he wondered, as Igor echoed him in the translator's lugubrious monotone. Eighth-grade history perhaps. Being in Russia made him feel all the more the patriotic American.

"There was a problem that later lead to the Civil War, but Jackson addressed it succinctly in five words. I repeat them now in reference to our two great nations as well as to our own great enterprise. Ladies and gentlemen . . ." He paused here to allow Igor to catch up with him. Of course, he could not ponder the accuracy of the translation, but the audience looked rapt. They began tapping at their goblets with their spoons, a lovely tintinabulation that underlined his final statement: "The Union must be preserved."

"*Soyuz nuzhno budet sohkranit!*"

THREE WEEKS later, the doorman at the building Alan lived in rang up to the tenth-floor apartment with a slice of park view. It was Alan Lapidus's retreat from the garment district and he often walked about as nakedly as Adam in the prelapsarian Eden. "There is a man here to see you, sir."

Alan wasn't expecting company. Nor was he in the mood for surprises. He had been downcast since his return from the Soviet Union. He missed the vibrant sense of participating in history that he had felt in the shadow of the Kremlin, and his treatment in Red Square was far superior to that he received in the vicinity of Times Square.

Three weeks before, the conquering hero had proudly stepped over the Weslacks threshold only to have his father greet him with the awful single word, "Knickers."

"Remember the knickers," his father cried, referring to the previous attempt the vice-president had made to bring Weslacks up to date nearly a decade before. Just out of college, Alan had perceived what he called a "fashion gap," and convinced his father to set out to rectify it. "Men wear shorts in the summer and long pants in the winter. What about situating knickers for the spring and fall?" They were still absorbing the losses, but what did regrets have to do with the price of ties?

Alan was already frazzled by a typical New York taxi driver who refused to take the route his fare suggested and got stuck in tunnel traffic. To make it worse, the man was a Soviet immigrant tainted by his adopted country's bad manners, scoffing at a two-dollar tip. Didn't he know that was forty rubles? Now this. His father continued, "We can't sell our own product. How can anyone make a market for Russian ties? Hey, I've got it. Instead of an alligator, we can put a bear on every item, like a status symbol. Ten thousand dollars. *Brrchhh!*" Mr. Lapidus screamed and went into a sort of fit. His hand pumped spasmodically until Alan realized that he was performing, miming, signifying. "Down the drain."

Nonetheless, the prodigal son remained convinced that by staking out a new geographical territory he would herald a new era of prosperity for Weslacks. He tied the knot of the tie that was to resuscitate the family fortunes, hardly realizing that it might as well have been a noose. The downpayment had been made, attorneys retained, and eighteen different signatures acquired to commence operations in the streamlined post-Perestroika, laissez-faire environment. Even the skeptical Lapidus elder had to admit that it was a strong start.

On the other hand, the reality of Soviet business never seemed quite so real once Alan was back in the States. Fax communications went unanswered. Shipping was a major obstacle, Customs a nine-foot hurdle. Nor did Ivan help much. He was ready to trade the nonexistent ties to the Philippines for sugar, the sugar to Indonesia for rubber. The rubber would be sent back to Russia to produce tires, the tires sold to John Deere for tractors. The tractors would return to Russia in exchange for advertising space in a right-wing Moscow daily, etcetera, until even Alan had to admit that the millennium was more likely to arrive before any profits. Over the previous month, all his expectations of making a killing dwindled to hopes of recouping his investment, until even these evaporated in the light of the harsh mercantile truth. "The deal's a stiff," his father cried. "D.O.A."

Alan was forced to take a nudist's asylum on the Upper East Side to escape from the endless recriminations that assaulted him in the garment district.

The doorman said, "He says that his name is Igor."

"Who's that?" Alicia inquired from her usual prone position, a hot compress across her forehead soothing her Tuesday migraine.

"My translator," he said.

"Your what?"

"My translator. The boy who translated for me in Russia. Maybe he can explain what I'm saying to you."

"Sir?" the doorman said.

In the pause, Alan had to decide if he wanted to see the embodiment of his failure, but he was already reaching for a bathrobe. The fellow had come from across the ocean and could not be denied. "Send him up, Ramon," Alan sighed.

It was Igor all right, wearing the same suit he had worn day after day in Moscow. At least it wasn't knickers. He also had two large suitcases, one of which he was opening as the elevator door shut behind him, to give Alan a can of caviar, an offering.

Although the younger Lapidus did not really know very well this man with whom he had spent the two most exhilarating weeks of his adult life, the foreigner's presentation was so artless that Alan was thrust back into his Soviet mood. He lost his New Yorker's inbred suspicion and embraced Igor. It seemed the proper welcome.

"You said that I should come to see you if I was in this country. I have sold the computer you have brought to me for eight thousand rubles for an airline ticket, so here that I am, the good businessman."

Alan worked the numbers. It was indeed good business to sell the computer for two years' salary. On the other hand, it was ridiculous to spend two years' salary on an airline ticket. The net result was a wash, no computer, no cash, the same as seventy years of Communism.

Alan was about to ask, "Where are you staying?" but when he saw Igor peering hungrily down the corridor that lead to the three bedrooms that would have housed three families in the Soviet Union, he knew the answer. Over tea he discovered that Ivan was not available to his brother. The pioneer Rogov, first to cross the wide Atlantic, was in California, his apartment inadvertently locked.

Igor said, "The key it was to be resting with All-Weather dry cleaners, but they do not know this. It must be an oversight." The only other address he had in New York was the residence of Alan Lapidus.

Jason, Alan's son, was at college, while Alicia spent more time at her lover's apartment than her home. The result was inevitable. Igor occupied the extra room.

The first thing Alan did the next morning was to give Igor some pocket money and a pocket to keep it in. If there was one thing the future master of Weslacks possessed in abundance, it was pants. He had cottons, khakis, and blends, bell-bottomed, straight-legged, stone-washed, pleated, cuffed, and corduroys with wide or narrow wales in every possible shade, from the top of the line to the bottom of the barrel, all in size 36. Of course, anything that fit Alan was wide on the undernourished Soviet figure, but Igor cinched them in with his black belt, and examined himself in the mirror. For the first time, Alan saw him as Ivan's brother.

"Okay, gorgeous. Let's go to breakfast," Alan said.

"As you wish."

Lapidus ate at the same coffee shop four days out of five. It was decorated with photographs of Mikonos, mock Tiffany lamps, and a revolving display case full of enormous coconut cream cakes that mesmerized Igor. They sat down and the waitress who knew Alan said, "The usual?"

Alan nodded and turned to his guest, "How about you?"

A look of fear came across Igor's eyes. "What do you mean?"

"What would you like to eat?"

"Whatever you wish."

"It's your stomach."

"Anything. What are you having?"

"Eggs, but that doesn't mean you have to have them. You can have pancakes or cereal or—"

"I will have eggs."

"How would you like them cooked? . . . I mean, they can be fried or boiled or scrambled—that is, mixed."

"I don't care. Whatever is simplest."

"Look, Igor, the cook doesn't care either, and he won't cook them unless you tell him how."

"But I—"

"It's your decision. Now make it."

Igor was terrified at the mere thought of choice. Then he had a brainstorm. "How are you having them?"

Alan looked at the waitress and said, "Make that two over."

The waitress looked at the stranger and asked him, "What sort of toast would you like?"

AT FIRST, it was pleasing to have a tenant occupying the room from which conspiratorial adolescent giggles and distressing narcotic aromas had seeped for years until Jason left to complete his so-called education. Alan particularly enjoyed a companion who was so un-failingly deferential in a way that Alicia had never been, not even in the early days of their marriage, and so appreciative of everything Alan took for granted. He loved watching his guest staring at fruit stands and he took a parent's pleasure in witnessing the fellow's growth. Within a week the foreigner managed to learn how to order breakfast at the Regency Diner by himself. It turned out that Igor didn't like eggs. He preferred oatmeal.

The only disagreeable moment occurred when Alan took his guest to the Weslacks offices without giving prior notice to either Igor or his father, and a raging Mr. L. hurled himself at the poor interpreter. "So where are the ties?"

Igor turned ashen.

"You led us into this, this trap, you son of a bitch. Why don't you go back to Dubrow's where you belong?"

"Who? Me?"

Alan said, "Dad, I'd like you to meet Igor Rogov. He was my translator in the Soviet Union. He's come to this country for a visit."

Mr. Lapidus huffed, "I thought it was Ivan."

"It's his brother."

Mr. Lapidus circled suspiciously around the visitor. "They sure are cut from the same bolt. Not like you, you, you"—he sought the ultimate insult and found it close at hand—"you second."

Alan did not need to be reminded that he had never quite measured up to his dead brother Robert's elementary-school promise. So what if he wasn't the world's sharpest businessman, the Rothschild of rags. He began to cultivate a new self-image as a philanthropist with the object of his beneficence ever-present for everyone to admire.

Igor was a great conversation piece. He was a curiosity, a political statement, and the embodiment of Alan's charitable impulses all in one six-foot swatch. The man's palpable need pleased Alan, and he positively enjoyed stuffing ten-dollar bills into his pocket like a mobster tipping a maitre d'. So what if the initial bad investment for the ties still rankled; this expenditure went straight to the moral bottom line.

All pleasures, however, wane if they are not continually made new. Like knickers, the novelty grows tiresome. Soon enough Alan's friends had heard the fried-egg story one time too many and began to think of Alan as a bit of a boob, as the translator whom nobody needed tarried.

Igor's plight was all the more pathetic because he would have been happy to leave Alan's umbrella, and to this aim he made awkward phone calls to a list of cousins of cousins, none of whom could offer more than advice. Afterward, he walked the streets in search of Help Wanted signs in shop windows, but nobody was willing to hire a man without papers, and so he trod sadly back to Third Avenue, practiced his woeful "Allo" on Ramon, and took the elevator up to the Lapidus aerie.

The heart of the problem was that Igor was hardly the most perfect object of charity. In his own way, Igor was effusive in his gratitude. His way, however, was less interesting than an inseam. Despite the Russian's lucky perch in the land of the free and the home of Wheatena, he acted no differently than he did in Moscow, depressed and consequently depressing.

In truth, Igor had decided that he wished to immigrate, but he did not have the slightest idea of how to accomplish this. Moreover, he had no knowledge of such basic Western skills as wielding a phone to get results. His brother, of course, was a master of the instrument, but Ivan remained out of sight in California—or was it Canada?—a mystery.

Alan took to making phone calls on Igor's behalf, quizzing attorneys on the arcane byways of immigration law. The simplest path was that of family reunification, and through the grapevine he learned that one could purchase a grandmother for fifty thousand dollars. Unfortunately for Igor, his host's bank account was not commensurate with his desire to rid himself of his unwanted guest. Alan investigated H-1 professional visas, and categories of desirability, and questions of asylum.

"When is he going?" Alicia whispered from behind the bedroom door on one of her infrequent nights at home. "This is driving me crazy." She was peevish because she was not used to being locked in with her husband.

"I don't know."

"Well maybe you should find out."

Alan shrugged. For a few days the fact that Igor disturbed Alicia was justification enough for his presence, but then Alicia ceased coming home on Tuesdays, bestowing her migraine on her lover, her husband supposed. Alan was left on his own with the dejected Slav. It gave him a bit of a migraine himself. He began to remember with great fondness his nights alone in the large apartment. At the time he had felt miserable, henpecked, father-dominated, gaining weight, but at least he had been able to walk naked, and he did not have to worry about which continent he was going to reside on or the KGB. In the face of Igor's pain, Alan's domestic problems now appeared self-indulgent.

Alicia called on the phone, "I mean, where is this famous brother of his?"

"I don't know."

The special occasion on which Ivan chose to communicate with Igor occurred while Alan was in the bath. He emerged, shaking the drops from his ears to see the translator hyperventilating on the couch. "Are you all right?" he asked.

"My brother called."

"Where is he?"

"In the background, I hear the sound of dishes, many dishes, clatter."

This sounded like it could have been Dubrow's, but Alan knew that Ivan was the kind of man who never moved backward. "What did he say?"

"He said I screwed up. What does this mean to me? He said that this is America, where there are no second chances."

"There, there," Alan felt as if he was comforting a child. "Is he coming back?"

"I do not know. He did not say. I did not ask."

That covered the subject pretty well.

Alan started directing the Russian outward, sending him to museums and movies, anyplace to be rid of his dismal presence for an hour. He put him on the subway to Brighton Beach, where the rest of the Russian community lived, hoping that he could find another place to stay, a job, information, anything.

Igor perceived his host's unhappiness. He recalled his first American's unbalanced euphoria in the Soviet Union, but Alan began to resemble a harried Soviet engineer more with each day, and Igor decided to cheer him up. The next morning, he studied the brilliant American kitchen appliances and produced a tray of fried eggs along with potatoes and toast and coffee and a small glass of orange juice, which he marched into his host's bedroom with pride. He had brought everything the Regency had to offer except a picture of a whitewashed Aegean chapel.

Alan pulled the sheets up to his chin. "What's this?"

"The usual."

Alan took the tray from the left side of the bed, swiveled it across his bunched up blanket, and dropped it off the right side, creating the same din that accompanied Ivan on the phone. While Igor scrambled to sop up the coffee and scoop up the eggs, Alan stepped into his bathrobe and said, "I didn't order this and I don't want it. I like the way I live and I don't need anyone to disturb my routine."

"I do not understand."

No wonder a nation of such people couldn't get it together to ship ties. Alan complained bitterly to his guest as if Igor was at fault for all of the flaws of the Soviet economy. He would have bought millions more ties if they had acted honorably. This would have put people to work, set dollars in motion. They were only harming themselves by not shipping Alan the ties he paid for. "They're mine!" he screamed.

In response to this diatribe, Igor merely stopped accepting money from Alan, and subsisted on a boiled potato a day. If Alan did not buy potatoes, Igor did not eat, but the less intrusive he attempted to be, the more his mere presence was intolerable. He cinched Alan's belt in another notch to wear Alan's pants.

When Alan finally built up the strength to ask what Igor's "plans" were, Igor said, *"Soyuz nuzhno budet sohkranit!"*

"What?"

"The Union must be preserved."

SHIVAH: SEVEN days of ritualized mourning required by Jewish law, a sort of open house in which others may pay their respects to the deceased and comfort the bereaved.

ONLY THE DAY before, Mr. L. had noticed a picture of a famous actress sporting a Soviet lieutenant's cap on the front page of the fashion daily. "It's a fad," Lapidus said before Alan had a chance to rub it in. "Like knickers. Someone's gonna sell a dozen and sit with a warehouse."

"I should be so lucky," Alan moaned, resolved to endure yet another day of his father's abuse at work and Igor's blue funk at home. Then Mr. L. keeled over, smacked his head on the edge of the gray metal desk, and died overlooking Seventh Avenue.

An ambulance came and all the piece workers lined the dingy hall to watch the body of the boss wheeled out.

Alan walked thirty blocks to his apartment for the first time in thirty years. The news, of course, preceded him.

Igor was on the couch when his host arrived. "I was sorry to hear from your father," Igor said.

Alan stared back, "So was I." The next thing he knew, arrangements had been made and half the world was milling about his living room.

Igor Rogov was an appropriate presence while the Lapidus family sat shivah. His perennially half-shaven countenance, his doleful manner, his slumped posture, were all the conventional images of sorrow. Although Jason returned from college and Alicia put in an appearance, theirs was neither the tan nor headache of true grief. Nor were they alone in the nature of their concerns. Over the course of the week, the secular world beyond the customary draped mirrors began to intrude. Cousin Rita pecked Alan's cheeks and told anyone who would listen about her son's career in podiatry. The neighbors nibbled a slice of honey cake and debated national politics with Lapidus's business associates, and even the rabbi from the synagogue that Alan's father had attended twice a year was ready to chat about the new television season after he had made certain that the family was not too distraught. At that point, Igor seemed to cast an aura of recrimination over the room.

Alan's apartment was more like a party where the guest of honor had yet to arrive than the chosen site for communal lamentation. Only Igor sat with his head in his hands, reminding them of their host's mortality and their own.

Alan was shaking hands with an accessories man, who murmured words of sympathy and began to feel out the future of Weslacks, when Alicia interrupted, "I mean, who does he think he is, a long-lost son?"

"Who?"

"Igor, the professional mourner."

Alan was about to try to answer it when they were all distracted by a telegram that arrived from Russia. "Tie deal looking good. Stop. Need dollars. Stop. Van."

Lord knew what Rogov was doing back in the USSR or what had happened to his much-vaunted reluctance to cross the Soviet border. Perhaps he was only able to return after he foisted his sullen brother off on Alan, the reverse of the Tzarist army's impressment of Jewish children. Instead of buying off his place with another body, Ivan was only able to assume that place after liberating someone from the grip of the Steppes. So the gullible American had not purchased a bulk load of silk ties, but his own human ball and chain.

Alan thought of his father's response to such a bargain, and caught himself before he laughed at an inappropriate moment. Let the buyer beware.

"Tie deal?" the accessories man peering over his shoulder asked. "Isn't that out of your line?"

"You're right. Here, you can have it."

"Really?"

"Yeah, if you make any money give ten percent to the Jewish War Veterans."

THE NIGHT his father was buried, Alan dreamed of him. The vision was so immediate that he was shaken awake by the power of his imagination, which was usually more intent on summoning pneumatic blondes displaying a variety of exotic lingerie. He sat up and looked at his surroundings. There was his wife, a rarer apparition in their nuptial bed than the dream blondes. There was his matching dresser and uncluttered end table and the unused exercise bicycle bought to siphon inches off his drastically increasing waist. He paced quietly and looked out the window. The park four blocks away was a deep tranquil green. He tentatively closed his eyes and saw his father again.

Alan padded to the kitchen, mixed himself a Scotch-laced milk, and returned to bed. As soon as he shut his lids, however, Lapidus the Elder reappeared behind the same desk he had died behind, and Alan could almost smell his cigar. It was more of a trance than a dream, a sort of hypnotic state. Alan was terrified, but so weary that he could not resist. His fingers clenched his quilt as the apparition barked in the Elder's normal Thursday voice, "What, you trying to avoid me?"

At first Alan was worried that his father would berate him for filial ingratitude or contracting a bad marriage or lacking common sense. He began to apologize for all the sins he had committed, but the dead man waved them off as minor indiscretions. "That's life."

"Thanks, Dad. So, um"—Alan did not wish to be blunt—"how are you doing?"

Mr. L. was not such a delicate soul. Though dead, he was clearly earthbound, more interested in the here and now than the hereafter. He had not bothered to return to warn his son about the perils of the netherworld or to entice him with the glories of eternity; instead, he told Alan where the will was hidden that divided up his stock between Alan and his two sisters.

"Thanks."

"Use Baumgarten for an attorney."

"All right."

"Oh, and one more thing. . . ."

"Yes?"

"Don't let the schmucks tell you not to smoke. When it's your time, brrrch!" He pumped his hand vigorously.

The next day, Julia arrived to pay her own shivah call, but Alan sent her straight back to the garment district with a curt, "Get to work, dear, and have a look under the radiator cover in the corner office. Bring back any papers you find there. It should take you about forty minutes unless you try to read them. Don't."

Of course, the trusted secretary knew about the hidden will. She was quite frankly amazed that the flaky ne'er-do-well Junior L. knew as much. He was, however, the new boss, just one more inequity of latter-day capitalism. Salaaming toward the elevator and wondering if Alan would demand the same gross sexual indignities as his predecessor, Julia said what she always did in similar circumstances. "Yes, sir."

Alan's father told him how to maintain control while seeing to it that the sisters received their proper due. The old man was surprisingly sensitive to his children's conflicting interests. Lapidus had definitely mellowed in the afterworld; he didn't even mention the cursed knickers once. Night after night he reappeared, eager to oblige his kin, to help. Death seemed to confer a benign elder-statesman status on the old crank.

Alan began to wear pajamas to bed out of respect. He who used to dread going to the office looked forward to the somnambular conferences with his progenitor. He kept a pad and pencil beside his bed to take down the received wisdom of twenty-five years in the business. He took down Julia's home phone number.

Their relationship was so much improved by his father's death that Alan even considered asking about his brother, but didn't. Maybe Robert was still a kid, a dead ten-year-old who was hard for a newly deceased single father to keep up with. Heck, even if Robert had grown up up there, he wouldn't have the kind of worldly knowl-edge of Seventh Avenue that Mr. L. and his second son shared.

All of this helped as the week of shivah came to a close. Alan began to ask advice on certain estate issues. "Should I sell the apartment?"

"Hey, in that world my crystal ball is no clearer than yours. Ask a broker."

Mr. Lapidus was more adept in his own field of fashion. He and his heir had discussions about plaids. Indeed, the last subject they spoke about on the dawn prior to the last day of the shivah was materials. He gave some cleverly pointed advice about the acquisi-tion of trimmings in a recessionary market, so that when the zipper rep approached Alan the following noon, Alan knew that the man was strapped for cash and that he could cut a better deal on the new year's supplies if he took advantage of the moment.

"So sorry to hear about your father," the rep said to Alan. "He was a giant in the industry."

"Just another size forty-four."

The man looked back in horror and realized that he was in the ring with a cutthroat.

"So, we're going to need five hundred gross this season."

The man could not bear to negotiate with an orphan who wore the ritually torn collar. He would have signed anything to escape, but just as Alan was grinding an additional twelve percent off the per-unit cost, Igor interrupted. He hadn't spoken a word in a week, but now he broke his silence. "Those zippers cost even more expensive in the Soviet Union, no."

A light hit the man's eyes as he realized the deal he had almost made, and he fled.

The new Lapidus spun about and stared at the interloper. It was one thing when Igor, whose no-goodnik brother Ivan did not even send a condolence note, promoted Alan's own failure, but when he interfered with the plans of the late, sainted Lapidus Elder—that was too much. Charity be damned. Alan exploded, "You're a jinx, a Jonah. I can't stand it. Get out of my sight. Hey, get out of my home."

"Out?"

"Out. Why did you come here anyway if it makes you so miserable?"

Asked a direct question, Igor responded with a direct answer. "The same reason you came to Moscow, to escape from your father. Only my father was the state. I needed to learn to become a man."

"Learn on your own. Out."

"Out?" The thought was totally foreign to Igor. The Soviet government may have mistreated its citizens, but it took care of them. There was no choice of eggs, fried or scrambled, in the morning, let alone white toast with creamy butter, but there was a stack of grainy crusts as tall as Abraham Lincoln in every store, and every citizen's belly was full. There was no choice of shoes, but nobody went barefoot. The Russians complained about housing, but they did not know the meaning of homelessness. Here, Alan Lapidus was his government.

"O . . . u . . . t. Scram, split, vamoose."

The tall young man retreated, an expression of horror on his face. "But, Alan, where can I go?"

"You should have thought about that before you decided to come, you elected to come. But it was a fixed ballot. What other Russian finds a room on Third Avenue?"

"But I have no place else."

"Go to Minsk for all I care."

Igor nodded and left the nicely carpeted living room, leaving only shallow depressions in the plush purple pile. Half the people stared at him, but those in the know were more inclined to stare at Alan with amazement and, perhaps, admiration, for his newfound authority. Alicia half-decided to remain the evening.

The afternoon wore on while Igor proceeded to pack behind the door exhibiting the lifesize poster of a rock star dressed in studded leather chaps clenching a bloody microphone in his fist. Finally, Igor placed a large fur hat on his head as he pulled the door shut behind him and strode silently through the hushed living room, like the Angel of Death leaving the premises. After he left, an estranged second cousin of the deceased asked, "Anyone got a deck of cards?"

THAT NIGHT, for the first time in a week, Alan had no dreams, and the next dawn he realized for the first time how badly he needed those dreams. For the first time since his father had died, Alan understood that his father was dead, and for the first time since he was a child, he loved the man. The pain of his loss was immense.

He woke with the taste of intestinal juice in his mouth. He jabbed his down-filled pillow into a comfortable hollow beneath his ear and shut his eyes, but sleep eluded him as remorselessly as it had previously compelled him. It was ironic that Alan had felt so comfortable in the USSR, 4,750 miles across the polar ice cap from his father's physical presence, whereas now he yearned for the man's spiritual aura, or whatever it was that left his bedroom smelling of cigars. But his father had left along with Igor. The damned Russian had stolen Mr. L.'s image, like an icon from an orthodox monastery.

The question then was where did the Russian go. Alan tore through the room that Igor had occupied without discovering a hint of his stay, not a scrap in the garbage revealing any of the obscure phone numbers he had dialed. The emptiness in Alan's dreams was echoed by the emptiness in his son's room. He opened the closet and the only garment hanging in front of Jason's old football jerseys was the pair of pants Alan had given to his guest as a gift.

He rummaged quickly through the pockets, but the only thing in them was a subway map Alan himself had loaned to the translator with the route to Brighton Beach outlined in black.

He took the elevator down to the garage only to find his car missing, on the road to New Haven with the son who had so graciously returned to New York for his grandfather's funeral.

Alan hailed a cab, but the driver refused to take him to Brooklyn.

"You have to. It's the law."

"So sue me, Mac. I don't cross the river, unless you want to go to the airport."

"Why should I want to go to the airport?"

"I dunno. Maybe you'll catch a plane to Brooklyn."

For a moment, Alan was uncertain. Then he looked down at the map in his hand and began running for the nearest subway to Brighton Beach. He had never been there, but he followed his own directions. It was a long ride under the financial district and across the Brooklyn Bridge, and then back underground. He grew fearful as every other white person left the train, but pretended to be immersed in a newspaper until the car popped above the surface within sniffing distance of the ocean.

Brighton Beach was an old station whose splintered wooden banisters had not yet been renovated to the sleek chrome sections of Manhattan. Alan rushed across the platform, through the turnstile, down the stairs, and onto the busy street where, for a second, he thought he might have returned to the Soviet Union. The signs were all in Cyrillic, and the first object that he noticed in one of the shop windows was a set of matryoshka, nesting dolls. He entered and inquired, "Excuse me, do you know a man, Igor Rogov. Tall, thin, pale face. He's an immigrant."

The proprietress was a kerchiefed woman so rotund that she looked like the prototype of the dolls. She replied, "So who isn't?"

No matter the disappointment, Alan continued to wander beneath the elevated track, buttonholing passersby to ask if they knew of Igor Rogov, pausing only when the train rattled overhead. There was clearly an element of hysteria in his behavior, because almost everyone he approached edged away in fright and stepped up their pacing to avoid him. Finally, a man selling newspapers from a stack on top of an empty milk crate said, "Yeah, I know the guy. He buys *Women's Wear Daily* a day late for half price."

"Where does he live?"

"What is this, a tour of the Movie Stars' homes? How do I know where he lives?" But seeing Alan's despair, the vendor took pity. "He goes in the direction of the Whiskey-a-Gogol. Maybe they know."

"Wh—"

"There."

Alan could hear the vibrato of accordions half a block away, across a sea of Cadillac roofs parked in the lot. The club itself was a boxy, cinder-block structure with a gaudy chandelier suspended from the tall ceiling in its lobby like a glass tornado. Three or four teenage valets wearing white shirts and black vests over their Weslacks jeans loitered in front, waiting to reclaim the cars for their owners; they reminded Alan of black marketeers.

The moment Alan arrived, the music suddenly stopped, but it had clearly issued from behind a pair of bronze doors shaped like the twin tablets of the Ten Commandments. Alan ignored the valets' scorn for anyone who arrived on foot and pushed the doors wide, entering into a ballroom that reminded him of the party room in Russia's Cosmos Hotel. The only thing that was missing was the faded square on the wall where the picture of Stalin was missing.

As was the custom in Moscow, the party had paused for a speech. A small boy wearing a knitted yarmulke with his name circling his curly hair was orating into a microphone. The boy spoke as slowly as if he expected a translator to repeat his words in another language. His high-pitched voice sounded like a cartoon character that Alan could not identify. He was saying something about learning to become a man. It was a Bar Mitzvah.

Alan did not remain to listen. He was keenly aware that he still ought to be in mourning, but he was on a sacred quest, seeking not amusement but the mystical resurrection of his father. He peered all about the great room, scanning the boy's parents and their guests until he saw a face that he recognized. It was Breitbart, a weird coincidence.

Next he scrutinized the waiters who were standing ready to wheel in carts full of raisin-studded coffee cakes and steaming samovars to celebrate the boy's coming of age. None of them were Igor, but they gave him an idea of where else he might pursue his quest. He slipped around the periphery of the ballroom and entered the kitchen, a dim, low-ceilinged space behind the bandstand, cramped with pots the size of barrels and gigantic mixing machines. A hundred plates were being scoured of chicken soup and prepared for the following day's mushroom barley. The only door exited onto the parking lot. There was no place else to go; the building was a single huge box on its foundation. Then Alan realized: there was a cellar. He plunged through the mists of the industrial dishwasher and down a narrow flight of stairs.

The basement smelled worse than the kitchen, a rank confection of yesterday's trash and the liniment and perfume of the employees' dressing area. The latter was approached by a narrow hallway further narrowed by boxes of wilted lettuce, its leaves like small green animals trying to escape from between the slats of their crates, yet a thin strain of music came from a room at the end. Alan approached and heard someone strumming on a cheap guitar, and singing, *"La cucaracha, la cucaracha / Ya no puede caminar,"* with a Russian accent.

The music halted the moment Alan opened the door. Igor was nowhere to be seen, but the long lost Ivan was leaning against the rough foundation wall, his long legs extending over the striped ticking and stray horsehairs of an unmade cot under the glare of a single bare bulb. Ivan was cradling the guitar and still stamping his feet while a tiny girl who could not have been more than thirteen years old danced for him, dressed in a training brassiere and flowery panties. At the sight of Alan in the doorway, the girl shrieked, reached down to grab a pink chiffon gown that rustled as it left the scabrous concrete floor, and dashed past him, returning to the party. Ivan said, "Spoilsport."

Alan scornfully quoted the telegram he had received, "Need money. Stop."

"Hey, Moscow, Brooklyn, what's the diff? I can have the guys here knock off ties that will beat the knickers out of Seventh Avenue."

Alan was disgusted. He wanted nothing to do with the sophisticate. He required only the hermit. "Where is Igor?"

"Ohhh, it is my brother that you want. Why didn't you say so?" The Russian's voice began to slow down like a record on a failing turntable, and then his eyelids drooped and his jaws, as if all of his features were suddenly subject to an intensified force of gravity. His skin seemed to grow thick and pasty. Then he ran his fingers through his hair and allowed a lank strand to drape across his forehead. His chin appeared to sprout stubble. "Allo."

Alan stared as he witnessed the transformation from one brother into the other. He realized that he had never seen Ivan and Igor together, nor had he ever spoken on the telephone to one while the other was present. "Who are you?"

"I do not understand," Igor intoned.

"I said, who are you?"

"Who do you want me to be?"

"Yourself."

Igor said, "Oh, but I only wish to be the good American. I am already learning your difficult, irregular language. I know to spell the one word, o . . . u . . . t."

"Look, I'm sorry about that. I apologize. I didn't know what I was doing and I don't care what games you've been playing with me. I want you to come home. I'm begging you. I'm beseeching you. I'm praying to you." More than Mr. L.'s life was at stake. Alan was pleading for the man's existence.

Igor ran his fingers through his hair with the motion of despair, but when he raised his head there was a sparkle returned to the young man's eyes. Ivan was back. He winked. "Say pretty please."

Alan said it.

Ivan became Igor again. "Are you sure that you wish for this? I do not care to be the intruder."

"No problem. Here, let me take your bags." The suitcases were empty; he was wearing his whole wardrobe. Alan walked down the damp hall that lead to the staircase up to the kitchen and out through the ballroom. Igor followed in his normal, desultory sulk.

Ivan returned only temporarily to wink at his teenage friend while Alan carried the luggage to the curb and flagged down a gypsy cab driven by another Russian who refused to leave Brooklyn until his fare promised to pay twice the figure on the meter.

Mr. L. never did return to his son's dreams, but two days later the first thirty parcels of silk ties arrived at the Weslacks mailing address. Igor went to the Soviet Union to manage the manufacturing side of the business, while Ivan moved in with Alicia in a penthouse down the block from Alan's place. The younger Lapidus said a prayer for his father once a year for the rest of his life.

The Golden Calf
and the Red Heifer

IF THERE is the tiniest discernible nick in the blade, the slaughter is considered unkosher. The animal may be dead, but its flesh is inedible by those who profess adherence to the first monotheistic faith. This stricture derives from a humanitarian impulse, for the being so nobly sacrificing its life and aspirations in order to satisfy the human appetite for flesh must be dispatched as painlessly as possible, so saith the law, which envisions pain commenced and concluded with the quality of the blade, eliding the fact that twenty-five hundred pounds of steer is shackled, hung upside down, and terrorized before the perfectly whetted edge is drawn in a single wild swipe across its throat. The law states what it requires and the rest is optional.

Removing the blood vessels to make the legal fodder more appealing, butcher Kleinberg pressed his own meaty fingers into the soft red flesh on either side of the gluey vessel that had once borne the fluids of life from the cow's hind quarters. While his left hand thus made an inverted V, his knife-wielding right incised a channel on both sides of the vein. He carved a deeper notch at the far end, and then, setting down the liturgical blade, gripped ahold and pulled the tube loose like a shoestring through half a dozen grommets. Then he cut deeper and divided the flank into two nearly equal halves. He lay the twin portions of London broil, $9.95 a pound, in the display case, like babies.

There were lamb chops to the left and steaks to the right of the London broil, and a conga line of connected short ribs, and a dozen chickens all heaped together in headless communion at the corner of the refrigerated coop. Various organs and tissues resided in two stainless-steel trays. There were soft, pool-shaped kidneys and wide, slimy slabs of liver. There were hearts and brains and pickled tongues from the speechless inhabitants of the gigantic freezer, which stood slightly ajar behind Kleinberg's back, its coolness refreshing in the summer heat that baked the rest of the shop as the sun came through the cracked windowpane with the Hebrew letters certifying Kleinberg's ritual credentials.

Despite the modesty of the blood-spotted premises, they were extremely profitable. The lone butcher in a community of Orthodox Jews was able to set his own standards and his own prices. The women of Spritzendyville did not even attempt to comparison shop. What could they do if his nearest competition was in the city forty miles downstate? Spritzendyville's residents were in voluntary exile from the urban melting pot that had welcomed their fathers. Here in the town named for a famous Colonial anti-Semite, they created their own regular Vilna in the Catskills, a ghetto of several hundred bungalows that sprawled north of Exit 112 off Interstate 17, sped past by more prosperous New Yorkers on their way to weekends in "the country." An essential portion of life in this historical village was flanken and Friday-night chicken soup. So what if the equivalent cuts at the local Finast mart were a third of the price that

Kleinberg charged. Finast maintained no intermediary between themselves and God.

Mrs. Schwartz, a dumpling from the canyon road, came to stock up on broilables. In the meanwhile, she poked her finger into Kleinberg's home-cooked derma to check the consistency. Wary of Kleinberg's thumb's tendency to rove onto the scale, she turned the trick around, leaning on the counter, subtly pushing up with the lower of her two chins the scale adrip with the juice of kine.

This was all part of the game as far as Kleinberg was concerned. Mrs. Schwartz gained the quarter-pound advantage she sought, but he mismultiplied the remaining 3⅝ pounds, and she never caught on. Although there were rabbinical briefs about weights and measures, such procedures were not explicitly enjoined in the kosher guidebook. Even if he hadn't used creative math to determine the price of Mrs. Schwartz's derma, he had tampered with the scale itself so that the weight of a pin feather was nearly a quarter of a pound.

Kleinberg cooked the rules in a dozen other ways. He inserted a syringe full of water into every breast. He knew the patriarchs' occult techniques for adding weight while subtracting volume. Worst of all, his blade was not quite as perfect as it ought to be. Fortunately, the eyes of the rabbi whose supervisory seal attached to Kleinberg's slaughter were not what they ought to be either. The rabbi's pocket, however, bulged whenever he left the shack behind the refrigerator, where the chickens and geese, lambs and cows of Sullivan County met their maker.

Kleinberg operated a vertical monopoly. He owned the herds, killed the beasts, sold their meat. He did everything but eat it. He was a vegetarian. Of course, this was his own darkest secret. He would be damned if he would let those morons who paraded under the banner of animal welfare know of his sympathy to their cause. He would take a rusty blade to them first.

No matter the bleats of the bovine martyrs and their foul allies, Kleinberg willingly continued to decimate their ranks on behalf of the matrons of the isolated mountain community which maintained the ancient dietary laws with a discipline that lesser civilizations devoted to art and diplomacy. Spritzendyville's residents were continually on guard for impurity within the confines of their miserable shanties, where hordes of ill-clad children shared a room while double sinks and double stoves and double refrigerators and double garbage cans graced the kitchen, lest even the refuse of meat and dairy mix.

All of Kashruth derives from the single Levitical injunction, "Thou shalt not seethe a kid in its mother's milk," a tender prohibition that tacitly grants the doomed creatures a maternal sensibility. The numerous amendments to the codex that has blunted Jewish taste buds over the millennia developed through centuries of Talmudic commentary.

Do not ask what bird ever gave birth to a calf and why therefore chicken paprikash is taboo. Neither should one ask what Canaanite farmer found lobsters in the eastern Mediterranean. Just give thanks that when the fecund waters of the North Atlantic were harvested, lox were not shellfish. Fins and scales were acceptable. Cloven hoofs were not.

Looming in blood-smeared smock, the master of their gastronomical discontent, Kleinberg knew his customers' appetites better than they did themselves. He knew who liked their steaks medium and who preferred them rare. He knew who trimmed the fat, and who gorged upon its excess. He knew who gnawed the bone. He knew their ailments and traced many to his produce. Pliskin needed iron; his wife bought liver every Tuesday which he dissipated on Scotch and potato chips at Wednesday-night poker with Salz, who had high cholesterol. The latter's wife apologized for having to cut down on red meat and made up for it with extravagant purchases of milk-fed baby veal.

Kleinberg knew who had gout and who suffered from arthritis, and which crackpot diet was supposed to heal them. Although his customers' husbands prayed at the small shul down the road from Kleinberg's cottage twice every day, the women only saw Rabbi Fainshtein twice a year; Kleinberg they saw weekly. They had to; he refused to deliver. They found this quaintly old-fashioned. It made his chops taste like their mothers'.

Invariably Kleinberg would compel a long line of customers to cool their many heels while he interrogated the lady at the front, drawing out the confidences of the Spritzendyviller: who could not conceive; whose unwanted eighth daughter was on the way; whose husband was about to be fired by the discount electronics firm that employed most of the community's wage earners. One could not obtain so much as a single chicken wing without undergoing Kleinberg's trial by gossip. The ladies were compelled to mortify themselves before the temple of flesh before they were granted its sustenance. Only after they revealed their secret dreams and torments were they allowed to pay for the privilege. The more sophisticated compared the ordeal to psychoanalysis.

NINE RED heifers were born between Moses and the Destruction of the Second Temple that ushered in the banishment of the People of Israel from the promised land for two thousand years. Each heifer was an omen of such enormous significance that the most rigorous priestly inspection was called for. Even one white or black hair marring the perfect surface of its hide would render it useless to anyone beside a butcher. Only after a determination of true and complete redness was the beast ritually burned, its ashes used for the services that required the utmost purity. Mystical speculation declared that the tenth red heifer would be provided by the Messiah. Kleinberg was naturally interested in all such speculation.

Likewise, he was aware of the legends of the golden calf, although the creature worshipped at the base of Sinai could not have been more valuable than A-1 prime. He knew how, depending on which rabbi interpreted the words of the Torah, boons ranging from clouds of glory, to angelic crowns, to life everlasting had been denied the Jewish people for their worship of the golden calf. These thoughts carried him near to sundown, Friday, time to close for the Sabbath. All of his regular customers had long since taken their chickens home to bake when he was interrupted in his theological study by an unfamiliar voice that requested, "One tenth of a pound of London broil, please."

"Vat, you tithing with my merchandise?" he sneered, face deep in a volume of Hebrew lore.

He waited for the apologetic response, "I mean ten pounds," or the sniffle of obsequious poverty or the tinkle of bells attached to the door closing in diffidence or rage, but there was silence on the other side of the display case.

Finally, Kleinberg lifted his head, and saw the young woman waiting calmly for her order to be filled. She was not the kind he was accustomed to, neither mousy newlywed with a thin kerchief pulled low across her forehead, nor bulky stew maker. She was a shapely young woman, dressed in a Kelly green outfit with brass buttons that shone in the late afternoon sun. Her complexion was as clear as a Californian's, her lips practically apulse with blood that required no cosmetic assistance. Her hair was as red as meat.

"Slice it thinly please. I'm planning on steak tartare for supper," she said.

He wondered if she was Jewish, for gentiles occasionally patronized his shop under the illusion that kosher meat was of superior quality. Kleinberg sold overpriced lamb chops to a slothful novelist who lived in an aluminum trailer, Thomas Pipkin, who swore he wasn't Jewish despite his name, and veal to Randolph Jones, a black man who sold aluminum trailers.

"Fashteyst?" she said. "Understand?" which answered his unspoken question.

He cut the tenth of a pound and set down an additional slice for good measure. Then he looked in her eyes, and he added another slice. She kept his gaze locked, and he added another slice, before his intrinsic cheapness stopped him.

Embarrassed lest any of the regular customers he stole from had witnessed his weakness, he wrapped the package in brown paper, and handed it across the counter.

"Thank you," she said, her voice as clear as a bell.

Suddenly the butcher realized that he had not heard the tinkle of door bells when she entered his shop. "You're welcome anytime."

Kleinberg was distracted for the remainder of the afternoon. He could not keep his mind on his sacred studies. When Mrs. Minsky came in, in a rush to buy before Shabbos, he gave her an extra joint too, as if his hands had been compelled to generosity by the redhead's visit.

He tried to think who she could be, because Spritzendyville was an insulated community. He had heard that Leskov the Tailor had a daughter in Boston, but the needle-and-thread man was a scrawny *no-goodnik*; he could not possibly have sired such an apparition. He ran down the list of families that lived on the mountain, and considered their relatives, like Morganit's cousins in Australia. Perhaps they grew women like that down under, but she had no trace of an accent, not Australian, not Brooklyn, not Boston.

Steak tartare, raw meat thinly sliced, elegantly prepared, taken into that mouth, torn to digestibility by those finely pointed teeth, sliding down the gullet, past the twin bosoms straining against the green silk.

Kleinberg shut the store and ventured back behind the house to the barn. The rows of animals stared mournfully at him, as if waiting for him to choose the scapegoat who would pay the price for his discomfiture. He stroked the chin of the shy lamb he had taken to calling Molly, and lead her across to the rear where the shackles and trough lay.

Molly was an idiot, prancing vainly before the others, delighted by her temporary release from her restraints, oblivious to the end of the path of such freedom.

Kleinberg ran his finger along the blade until the flaw that only he knew of caught on the ball of his thumb and brought a drop of blood to the surface. He smeared it across his apron where no one could tell the B-positive from the more livestockish types. He hung Molly up, ignoring the pathetic eye contact the upside-down lamb attempted to make with the man who had housed her, named her, fed her, and been her benefactor, and who now slit her throat and jumped back lest his canvas soles be soiled by her blood.

Rabbi Fainshtein spoke that evening about the "sins of the people" that had lead to the Babylonian exile. Inspired by the prophet Jeremiah, he attained a pitch of unusual fervor, and Kleinberg decided to contribute more than he had already pledged to the community's day school.

The redhead returned at the beginning of the following week and requested several ounces more than she had on Friday, this time in the shape of a "lamb kidney." Kleinberg had whetted her appetite. He gave her the organ he had removed from the still quivering body of Molly that first afternoon. As she left the shop, he noticed that she was wearing deerskin boots, their fringe hanging down about her ankles. He also noticed her knees.

When she returned the next day, her hemline was higher, her neckline lower. Yet the more she revealed, the more she requested from Kleinberg. "Half a pound of bacon."

"You mean beef fry," he suggested—the strips of cured steak that simulated pig on the griddle.

"I mean bacon," she said.

He was shocked and replied, "I can't provide that. You must try the Finast in Monroe."

"All right," she said, and started for the door.

"Wait." This time he did not allow the bell to ring.

She turned, and the shape of her breast was outlined underneath the diaphanous silk shirt that she wore with such fetching negligence.

He thought of all the shortcuts he took in his business, and in particular he thought of the knife that he had not bothered to replace because a quality slaughtering blade cost fifty dollars. In that instant, he made a deal with God, that if he was allowed to bring this woman the *trayf* she desired, he would spring for a new knife. It was a dubious bargain, and he knew it, but he grabbed the deity's outstretched hand anyway, and shook.

The moment a red heifer was born, the priestly caste leaped into action. Their entire ministry was justified by this fabulously rare beast which sanctified all those fortunate enough to bask in its presence. The ashes of the red heifer were used to atone for the myriad sins of a nomadic people still tentative in their embrace of the harsh Hebrew covenant. It provided the absolution that a later generation would find in the confessional of Rome. Kleinberg the mundane butcher felt himself to be in the presence of the sublime. He had no choice but to follow the heifer wherever it lead.

WEDNESDAY MORNING, Kleinberg stepped into his pickup truck with the sign of the axe on its door and manure staining the rear cab. He filled up at Mordecai Wexler's gas station and drove forty miles, crossed the Delaware at Oheka, and continued south until the terrain flattened and he arrived in Pennsylvania Dutch country, where he stopped at the first picture-postcard farm he saw. It had a red barn, a white shingled house, and a picket fence.

"Allo," a pale-faced man greeted him.

"I would like to buy a pig."

"Not for sale."

"I have money." He thought of the Jews in the wilderness who had turned over their gold to mold the infamous calf.

The farmer looked at him with a penetrating, suspicious gaze.

"I do not usually travel to buy animals. . . . I am not familiar . . ." Kleinberg stammered. He didn't know the proper price nor the features to look for to determine value, whether it was the condition of the teeth, the wear and tear on the feet, or the curl of the tail. But the butcher knew how to kill. He had his knife in a leather sheath beneath his long coat.

"Where is your yarmulke?" the man asked.

"I—I didn't wear it," Kleinberg confessed as he rubbed his hands nervously back along his temples. He didn't realize that his hair was permanently matted by the thin black skullcap that was the first article he donned every morning except today, but he did not question how the man knew that he was Jewish. He assumed that the mark was written on his forehead as clearly as Cain's. He tried to explain that what he was doing was wrong: "For myself to buy, I mean—not for you to sell. No offense."

"Five dollars," the man said.

"A pound?" Kleinberg asked.

"No," the man said. "Five dollars."

Kleinberg opened his wallet.

The man pointed to a white rock on his lawn and said, "She's all yours."

Kleinberg looked at the rock, and discerned the flattened ears riding back across the pink pate. He approached the sleeping beast and reached down to claim it.

Suddenly there was a squeal, and the thing ran snuffling into the backyard.

He looked at the man at the door, who repeated, "All yours," folded the five-dollar bill into his pocket, and added, "if'n you can catch her."

Kleinberg took the knife from its sheath. The pig would not mind the flaw in the blade. The animal now rooted about under a child's swing hung not quite parallel to the ground under a shady elm tree. The professional butcher was like a maniac pacing about the yard, knife in hand, until he pounced, and came up with a mouthful of pig slop.

The intended victim rushed behind the laundry hanging on the line, amidst the drooping leaves of a willow tree. Kleinberg continued to track his prey. Once, the knife caught onto the side of the pig as it scooted past the butcher. The beast turned and stared at him with its pink eyes, and a thin red line appeared on its flank like invisible ink emerging on white paper. He pounced again and the knife penetrated the pig's rear to about a half an inch in depth before the beast escaped, the blood smeared across its haunch this time, and dripping into the dust.

Kleinberg was exhausted, but if he could not outlast a pig, how could he expect to win a woman? He readjusted the knife in the palm of his hand and set out to stalk the creature. He cornered it between a storage shed and an upended wheelbarrow, and saw the smile of the seller through the screen door. The pig burst leftward in a desperate bid for freedom, and Kleinberg instinctively dropped in that direction. For a second his body lay sideways across the pig's broad back, like a saddlebag, with one arm hooked about the creature's neck.

"Ride 'em, cowboy," the man at the door laughed.

The pig's rear legs temporarily splayed, but regained their upright position and struggled to escape. Kleinberg brought the knife about and started sawing ineffectively at the neck. Unfortunately a pig's neck is about as wide as an ironing board. Blood dripped, flowed, and spurted, yet the swine dragged the butcher in a jerky zigzag, all the while squealing its intentions to continue living.

Kleinberg retained his desperate hold, sure that if he let loose the pig would disappear forever. Still sawing, he finally severed an artery, and felt the hot blood gush over his scraped fists, and he rode the dying beast until it collapsed, all his.

"HOW MUCH?" Kleinberg's special customer asked when the kosher butcher proudly presented her with his quarry.

"Five dollars."

"Very fair."

"As yourself."

There was no mention that the strips of meat on the scale would have ruined him instantly and completely if their origin had been made public. A knife was one thing, but even blind Rabbi Fainshtein would not have been able to ignore the pointed ears under the counter.

"How do you cook this?"

"I thought you knew."

"I thought you could help."

Kleinberg led her to his kitchen just the other side of the walk-through freezer. Like every other kitchen in Spritzendyville it was enormous in order to accommodate two of each appliance. She placed the strips of fat side by side across the surface of a cast-iron frying pan.

Kleinberg stifled a feeling of nausea as the fat began to sizzle, and tiny droplets of grease bounced around the pan until they burst and were absorbed by the metal. He thought that he would have to discard the utensil that had served him so well, cooking eggplants and grilled cheese sandwiches through the decades.

"This will take a while. I like it crisp."

"Yes."

"It develops more sweetness that way."

Here he was, a man who could not bear the taste of the hamburgers he disseminated throughout the devout shtetl in the mountains, discussing the flavor of pig. But he thought of the new knife he had promised himself and repeated to himself that it was a sacrifice he was making in order to present the community with a more sacred tool.

The woman turned toward a flight of stairs that lead to the bedroom the butcher had carved out of the attic over his shop. He looked at the old blade lying in the plastic rack beside the double sink, the left portion of which had never been used until that day. Kleinberg had scoured the blade again and again in a vain attempt to expunge all trace of pig from its notched surface. Still the aroma lingered. He turned back. She was gone, upstairs.

Kleinberg had never been married, although he was considered a very desirable catch by the widows of Spritzendyville. He was strong and he was rich and, aside from minor violations of the few arbitrary laws that related to his profession, he was pious. He obeyed all of the laws that he could, some of which mandated a separation of the sexes, like meat and dairy. He followed the redhead.

The sputtering grease in the kitchen caught fire as her green skirt fell to the ground.

Kleinberg, however, was too dizzy with passion to realize what was occurring outside the cramped bedroom. He quickly disrobed, setting his ribbed undershirt atop his jacket and pants, and removing the ritual fringes that called to mind the presence of God, who knew what a sinner he was.

Less than an hour later he was roused by shouts outside his window and the heat that he had thought was self-generated coming from the other side of the bedroom door. The door itself seemed to disappear before his eyes, a tiny red hole rapidly expanding to engulf the entire threshold.

The window was smashed by well-meaning firefighters.

"Kleinberg. Kleinberg, are you there?" he heard the voices shouting.

"I am here," he cried, and tried to shake his companion awake.

"Hurry. The roof's caught."

"Yes, yes," he said, still shaking her, too distraught to be surprised that his would-be saviors did not appear to notice his companion. "Hurry," he repeated their plea.

But the redheaded woman's only response was a languid grin that took full cognizance of the flames breathing into the room as if there was a steam bellows powering them from the other side. "Forget me," she said. "Think of the other animals."

The house was a wreck, yet Kleinberg's stock was precious. He tried to dash through the flames, but was rebuffed, and the hairs on his chest singed bitterly. Only then did he smell the burning meat below, burning cows, burning lambs, and burning chickens, both living and dead, those in the barn and those in the freezer. He was sure that the ice in the display case had long since turned to steam while licks of flame lit the sky. He smelled burning pig.

"Here, Kleinberg!" Rabbi Fainshtein was perched on the ladder thrown against the blazing shingles.

The butcher ran for safety. Together, he and his rescuer crashed to the earth where Kleinberg, clad only in a blanket that some charitable soul wrapped about his shoulders, sobbed uncontrollably while the house and shop continued to burn until there was nothing left to feed the flames.

ASHES AND rubble and charred joists and melted chrome and broken glass covered the site of Kleinberg's Kosher Grocery and the scent of burned flesh inhabited the rest of Spritzendyville like a plague of locusts.

The whole town had gathered to share the loss; the previous evening's repast was the last meat they would eat for months. The leader of the communal self-help society tried to comfort the still-grieving butcher. "There, there, all is not lost. Here—" Minsky picked up the one item that remained intact amid the rubble.

Kleinberg was suddenly as silent as the bones of the creatures who had perished in the fire.

"Take it, to start with, a foundation to build upon." Before the man handed Kleinberg the blade, he idly rubbed it, and cried, "Ouch."

"Hey, look." The people circled in for a closer examination of the blade with the tiny triangle notched out an inch from the tip.

"It's not kosher."

"Anyone can see that."

"It must have been damaged."

But the rest of the blade was untouched by fire. Even the wooden handle had miraculously avoided being consumed in the flames.

It was clear that rather than being the result of the fire, the unkosher blade was the cause of the fire. Blame began to hover in the air like smoke above the ruins.

"Not only does he violate kashruth, he endangers the welfare of the entire community."

"What if the fire spread?"

There was a harshness and a resentment built up of years of surrendering to Kleinberg's outrageous demands. As soon as one matron realized that the butcher was vulnerable, so did her neighbor.

"That chicken I bought last week didn't look very healthy."

"Your veal was stringy."

And always they returned to the knife, which they passed about the circle, and each one who held the weapon brought a drop of blood from the tip of one of his or her fingers and felt newly powerful enough to accost the man who had cowed them all.

"Four pounds of chopped meat I bought, it made three hamburgers. Four pounds."

"My first son should have weighed that much."

"Look," the rabbi cried as he held the guilty weapon up to the fallen butcher's eyes.

The man of flesh looked at the man of spirit and said, "It is holy."

"It doesn't look holy."

"None of you understand," Kleinberg wailed. He gestured to the ashes of the red heifer spread as loam to repent the sins of the past and to mitigate the sins of the future.

"No," Rabbi Fainshtein agreed. "We don't understand." He twisted the angle of the blade and winced as his own blood joined his congregants'. "Only you understand."

That was true. Only Kleinberg understood the inherent morality of flesh, its weakness and its strength. Only Kleinberg, who had sinned in the midst of sanctity, was now capable of finding sanctity in the midst of sin. And the only way he could prove this was to make one last sacrifice. He grabbed the knife from the rabbi before any of them could stop him. Tranquil in the certitude that he had already atoned for his sins, because all the hairs were red, even those for which only he could vouch, Kleinberg made payment in full, one last stroke with the blade which, when it fell to the ashes, was as straight as the line from Adam to Moses.

The Devil and the Dutchman

RABBI ELIEZER Vandemeer, too faithful son of frugal Dutch merchants, traders in argyle, accumulators of low country acreage and fine seventeenth-century engravings, did not look forward to his annual visit to his family's demesne. Although he never enjoyed his sisters' ritual excoriation of him for abandoning the family's fruitful mercantile endeavors in favor of the rabbinate, this trip made his bunions throb with more than their daily intensity. He was an embarrassment to the secular dynasty which had been shaping Dutch commerce since Johannes, the first Vandemeer worth mentioning, extracted the ambergris from the intestines of the whales that washed up on the front doorstep of his cottage in the days of William of Orange. Great-grandson many times removed from that original dynast, Eliezer was born to a position that the study of Talmud did nothing to satisfy.

The rabbi was uncomfortably settled in a small town in New England, America, thousands of miles from the Vandemeer factories that cornered the continental argyle market to the consternation of the austere Scotsman whose native product the industrious Vandemeers had usurped. Withers, Connecticut, was all postcard village green: hardware store, home-baked pies, and Unitarian church. The rabbi's so-called congregation there was composed of wealthy week-end New Yorkers, similar, he often thought with ironic detachment, to his family.

The synagogue operated out of a square cinder-block box erected in two weeks flat at the perimeter of an empty shopping center. It was intended as a bank, but was temporarily donated to the congregation as a tax dodge by the insolvent developer, hopeful perhaps that God in the guise of the good Dutch man of the cloth would smile upon him and grant him the tenant on whose behalf it would be worth evicting his angel. It was a Reform synagogue, of course.

The rabbi had been run out of Holland by his keen faith, yet found himself shunned by his more religious compeers in the new world for lack of the necessary orthodoxy. He found a home in the apostatic movement that allowed his infrequent parishioners to drive to the shopping center, park anywhere they liked in the empty acres paved for shoppers had there been stores to serve them. They left their expensive foreign cars at the distance they felt they needed to walk to sate their own notions of propriety, those from more Orthodox backgrounds parking at the far end of the site, beside the structure built to the specifications of a supermarket which would have driven Ma Cummins's pie shop out of business had it ever managed to get into business itself.

Precarious though his pulpit clearly was, it suited Vandemeer. He lived in isolated contemplation in the area wishfully intended for the bank's vault, and wandered the empty space of the nonexistent pizza parlor, party shop, and video store, vaguely looking out for his bankrupt benefactor's good. The roof leaked, and he attempted to patch it, but ended up with more tar on himself than on the seam of roofing paper that had warped and allowed a continual stream of rainwater onto the concrete floor of the would-be Chinese restaurant. In the summer, mosquitoes bred there. Then he returned to the comfortable, premechanical era of the sages and their musings on found objects no less removed from the daily life of idyllic Withers than the spewings at the argyle works outside of Rotterdam.

Weekends, Rabbi Vandemeer tended the desultory spiritual cravings of his tribe, chatted with the ladies wearing the latest in country fashion, and sadly waved to them as they trod across the parking acreage to drive off to a round of golf to which he was not invited.

Come winter, even this remnant virtually disappeared, until his one regular parishioner was Irving Bensonbaum, his patron. Fat Irving came to sadly survey his folly and to seek ease in the guidance of the one human being who undoubtedly loved him.

Bemoaning the fate that had left him with only rabbinical consolation, Bensonbaum confessed, "Sometimes I think of jumping off the roof."

Of course the sprawling building was only one story, but Irving might have severely sprained his ankle. Besides, it was far more likely that he would fall through the rotting structure. Nonetheless, Rabbi Vandemeer took the landlord's complaint seriously, and reiterated the conventional wisdom that God's ways were not for man to comprehend.

"It's not God's ways I want to understand; it's the real estate market."

"That too is mysterious," Rabbi Vandemeer solemnly replied.

"I mean, the demographics are perfect. Average income forty grand, plenty of discretionary capital, a fair density once you add up all the villages in a ten-mile radius, no competition except for that goddamn square. I've got six slots per thousand feet, and you can't park anywhere near that forsaken hardware store—have you tried?"

Rabbi Vandemeer did not own a car but walked two miles to provide himself with the minimal necessaries of life, Ma Cummins's bread, toilet paper, and frozen orange juice.

"Ah well, take care, Rabbi," Irving sighed, and set off for the latest in a series of meetings with his bankers, who were "restructuring his portfolio," which really meant stripping him of every last asset he had accumulated during better seasons.

Once Irving had left, the rabbi felt a chill that aggravated the terminal ache in the corns that his family's socks had never been able to alleviate. He thought it was punishment for their sins, and he bore it stoically, limping downstairs to check out the boiler that Irving insisted it was the rabbi's responsibility to maintain.

Stepping gingerly off the bottom stair, before he could reach for the switch to illuminate the dark basement, Eliezer Vandemeer walked into a vast pool of reeking black liquid that seeped through the foundation of the building, accumulated in the shallows beside the boiler, and ran through a crack in the other side. At first, he thought it was oil from the boiler. Wading through the iridescent muck to search for the valve to shut the awful flow at the source, he was astonished to discover two things. First, the boiler was powered by gas. Second, the corns that had nearly crippled him had ceased to hurt.

The oil must have soaked through the open flap in the soles of his ancient loafers, very much like the seam in the roofing, and soothed the corns, lubricated them.

There was a lesson to be learned, he thought, as he pondered the situation, something about a silver lining, and he could not be too unhappy with the incredible cleanup that loomed as long as his feet were pain-free. He delayed the cleanup, vaguely guilty about his tenantly obligation, but too comfortable to do anything but stroll into town and enjoy a blueberry muffin.

When the corns reappeared a week later, the rabbi assumed that another bathing in the weird seepage might help, and it did. He peeled off his blue-and-green regimental Highlander hose and waded into the soothing balm, which was more efficacious than he could have imagined. When he rubbed it into the space between his toes, he watched with disbelief as the paper cut that had sliced his thumb turning pages of Rashi the evening before spontaneously shriveled and closed.

He looked more carefully at the seepage. He filled a bucket and climbed the ladder to the roof, where he spread the gooey stuff over the gaps in the black paper. They too seemed to cleave to each other and without having to wait for the next rain, he knew the leak had been sealed.

It was a fine season in his life, that winter. Between ritual immersions in the mysterious black fluid, a kind of inner peace descended upon Rabbi Vandemeer. It was a feeling he had not known since he first discovered the God of his fathers in the tiny synagogue his ancestor had endowed but never attended off Kaltenrue.

A month later, he was still sitting in the basement, which might as well have been the spa at Saratoga, his feet and the feet of the rickety chair that was now solid, soaking in the restorative solution. His pencil was running under the lines of the text propped in his lap when he realized an interesting sidelight to Maimonides's notion of the attributes of God. He reached down to annotate the text when the tip of the pencil snapped.

Rabbi Vandemeer was so comfortable he didn't want to go upstairs, so he dipped the tip of the pencil into the inky muck and began writing.

Rabbi Vandemeer's script was usually illegible, yet this time the lettering flowed effortlessly across the page, spreading to encompass a large, ornately embellished capital and the rest of the letters. More incredibly, the language itself seemed to flow. Usually, the pages of his notebook seemed a daunting expanse of heavy white bond, but this time he easily conquered it. The ink itself seemed to compel a literary as well as visual virtuosity.

It was at this point that Rabbi Vandemeer wrote a letter to his family, Margaret, Eugenia, and Sue, the three weird sisters. He had no one else to communicate with but these women, who had made it clear that until he was willing to assume his proper responsibilities in the family firm, they had no use for him. But he had to tell someone that he had discovered the elixir of perfection. This task would have been impossible a week ago, but suddenly he had the tools at hand; his very willingness to consider such an undertaking was astonishing; his ability to achieve it was absolute proof.

After the letter to Holland was written, he commenced a sermon for his usual audience of three, just for fun, and the magical substance continued to astound. The connections between the word of the Lord and the everyday world became apparent between the tips of his fingers and the nib of the pencil without once seeming to pass through his mind. Had he really made the clever analogy between the Temple scapegoat and the contemporary political scene? Had the revelation as to the role of the Jew in today's society sprung full bloom?

Rabbi Vandemeer sighed. It was the best sermon he had ever composed, but he knew that he would never have the power to deliver it as stunningly as it had been written. The rabbi's hesitant, stammering sermonizing was a disgrace, but he had an inspiration. He held his nose; he closed his eyes; he took a sip.

Now he orated with the elocution of a suburban firebrand, a prophet, a poet like Dylan Thomas in his cups, a rolling charming brogue, improvisation further modifying the words on the page. He was enjoying himself, strutting back and forth in the oily wash and declaiming with a power he had never been able to muster in front of an audience, when he realized he had an audience after all. He turned to the person standing on the bottom stair, an elderly man wearing a gray uniform with his name written in script over his chest. "Very nice," the fellow said.

"Who are you?"

"Boiler repair."

"The boiler's not broken."

"I got a complaint here," the man said, waving a pink slip.

Rabbi Vandemeer suddenly felt protective of his magical wellspring. "It's a gas boiler. Somebody must have made a mistake."

"No mistake," the man said. "Look at this stuff. Valve's right over there."

Next to the chair, where he would have seen it easily, there was a bright red turn-off switch. "Okay, then, I'll take care of it," the rabbi said.

"Nope, I've got to do it. Job's a job. Feel that way yourself, Rabbi?"

"How do you know I'm a rabbi?"

"Who else would be down here in the dark, Rambam on his lap, ranting about God."

"How do you know what I'm reading?"

"I'm one of the Chosen People myself."

The man did not look Jewish, but neither, presumably, did the fair-skinned, red-haired rabbi.

"Look," the rabbi said, "this is private property and I'm afraid that I'm going to have to ask you to leave."

"Very private property," the man said, diving into his clipboard and emerging with a deed and full authorization for his labor.

The rabbi was desperate. "Look," he said, "I really need this to stay here. I'll sign anything you want, but please go away."

"Anything?" the man said, looking through the clipboard again. "Say, perhaps a statement that you've been worshiping illicit deities."

The rabbi looked more carefully at the intruder. "Who are you?" he asked again.

The man smoothed out the patch over his chest. The green script read, "Lucifer."

"Nooo!"

"Yep. The man himself. In the flesh. Come to collect, that is if you're inclined to make a deal. Will the contestant in the gabardines come on down and pick door number one, door number two, or door number three."

TAR, PITCH, the Devil's own soup. Lucifer leaned against the boiler and steam rose from his clothes as he discoursed, "You see, it's the craving for perfection that brings on deviltry. One can rest content with God's failures or one can seek to rectify them. Physical flaws are the easiest to take care of, baldness, breastlessness, you name it. Then there are the failures of commerce or philosophy, ills of the body and ills of the soul. Of course, it's up to you what you most wish to repair."

True tender of his flock, Rabbi Vandemeer's first thought was for the most unhappy person he knew. "Do you think you could do something for Irving?"

"Who do you think arranged financing for this elephant?"

"This was a favor?"

"No, it was a deal. Irving had his demographics. All he asked for was the money to build the damn thing. If he had wanted tenants that would have been a different deal. The man made a business judgment. I'm invested in the Sun Belt myself. Talk about bad timing."

"But—"

"Hey, I don't have any crystal ball. I get lots of advice, mind you, but it's not always good."

"So . . ."

"Yes, yes, I'm going through a little restructuring myself. But you know, you turn up the boiler a few notches and as soon as the bankers start to sweat, I can usually come to terms."

The rabbi stared in astonishment.

"I know. I know. Everyone thinks I can get anything I want, but that's not true. I cannot create ex nihilo. I can, however, fix what's broken. You can think of me as sort of a fixer, like those guys down at the waterfront. Sometimes I sub out work to them. My real forte is to encourage the lack of trouble, to grease the wheels as it were."

The rabbi was skeptical. "So it's just a universal lubricant you've got your paws on. WD-40 for the soul."

The Devil said, "You think it comes cheap. When I was a lad—"

"Wait, I mean, I thought that you had nothing like an ordinary childhood."

"Ordinary, it wasn't."

"I meant like any sort of a childhood."

"Don't be silly, everyone does. I was a boy like you were a boy, back in Strasbourg in the twenties."

"The nineteen twenties?"

"Sure."

"But you've been around forever."

"Not precisely. I was an idea whose time had not yet come for millennia. You can track demonic imagery to Bel Marduk in Babylonia, or further back to Neanderthal drawings if you're anthropologically inclined. Now maybe there were other devils. I don't know, but this century was the time you could say I came into my own. My mom used to warn me about it."

"You had a mother?"

"Doesn't everyone?"

"I suppose so."

"What you're failing to comprehend is that I was a person like anyone else. I became a devil, *the* Devil."

"How?" Vandemeer was fascinated.

Then the devil really amazed him. "I found a spring," he said, "of bubbling oily stuff."

"Hmm."

"But I was a giving kind of boy, generous to a fault. Rather than use the stuff for myself I used it to serve others, so the gift was not limited by my own psychology, but self-perpetuating in the dreams of others."

"What sort of dreams?"

"That is the crux, isn't it? Of course, this century had fertile ground in which to plant my seed. I remember most vividly my first disciple, a young painter in Austria. Glory years, indeed. I moved from strength to strength, ranging eastward into the Caucasus. Georgia, a young lad with a wisp of a moustache. India/Pakistan nineteen forty-eight. China and the Cultural Revolution. I get around."

At this point the image of his own future struck Vandemeer: Shy Rabbi Vandemeer becomes an orator of stunning power, a writer, a healer, a miracle maker. Was he doomed to tyrannize nations?

As if reading the rabbi's mind, the Devil said, "Not necessarily. You see, it depends on the ground where the seed lands. Some, take your buddy Bensonbaum, use it to mundane ends; his was the elixir of finance. Others use it to woo beautiful women, a drop in their champagne, you can imagine the rest. Hot stuff. Your use has been most interesting, my dear Vandemeer, perhaps the most interesting since my own. Would you like to continue with my product?"

Was this the offer?

The Devil said, "Of course, you can return to the pallid simulacrum of life you've come to expect. I can turn the valve and send some fellows to clean up your basement in the blink of a bat's eye."

It was pretty eloquent lingo. Perhaps the Devil had taken a nip of the elixir himself.

"They'll organize your library, too. I'll throw that one in on the house."

Vandemeer was embarrassed. His library was a shambles; he had meant to get around to it, but never had the time. Volumes tumbled over volumes. Ancient commentaries were stacked upon rabbinical tracts, packed in trunks, heaped in the corners of the vault, some of them quite rare manuscripts he purchased with his share of the stocking proceeds at the bibliophile auctions in Ghent. The prize of his collection was a rare sixteenth-century gloss on Maimonides he purchased from a street vendor in Antwerp during a stopover on his annual visit to his sisters. Now that he thought of it, the Devil looked familiar. . . .

"I told you, I get around."

"Let me think about it."

"Sure, no problem, you've got twenty-four hours."

THAT NIGHT, the rabbi trod to the end of the parking lot where a pay telephone booth acted as a mosquito trap. He dialed his landlord's home number that was meant only for emergencies.

Bensonbaum was clearly drunk when the rabbi finally reached him on the tenth ring. "What's the matter?" he growled.

"Well," Eliezer didn't know where to start. "There's an oily seepage in the basement."

"Keep away from him," Bensonbaum shrieked into the phone.

"So you understand what I'm saying?"

"I'll be right there." Bensonbaum hung up.

"Right there" meant a two-hour drive, but the inebriated land-lord was in Withers in an hour and fifteen minutes, his car spinning wildly into the lot and screeching to a halt in front of the empty bank like a crazed peddler desperate to make a midnight deposit.

The rabbi was sitting calmly in his library, manuscript on his lap. "Come, let us study," he said, as placid as he had ever been in his life.

Bensonbaum tried to tear the volume from his hands, but his grip was unsteady, he lost his balance, and fell into one of the folding chairs set up for the tiny congregation.

The chair tottered, but held his weight. He wiped his forehead. "It's bad, Rabbi, worse than I could imagine. He wants not only my soul, but my rabbi's. You're the only authentic thing in my life."

Vandemeer mulled this over, and said, "The role of the rabbinate has undergone a very curious transformation in this country. In Europe, rabbis were merely those with a bit more than average familiarity with the sacred texts. Here, one is expected to be a kind of intercessor with the deity. Of course, that is traditionally the role that priests have within the Catholic church." He felt pleased with this analysis and thirsty for more of the stuff that enabled him to think this way.

Bensonbaum accused Vandemeer of the truth. "You've been drinking it, haven't you?"

"Today's on the house."

"It's like schoolyard pushers. That's how he gets you hooked. With me it was a sweetheart deal on a two-family house in Bridge-port, below market rates, no points, the appraiser was eating out of my hand. I went on to larger things, and then I saw this parcel, sweet, raw land, sewer and water easily available and a crying need for—"

Vandemeer finished the sentence, "—An empty shopping center."

"Hey, maybe there was only a need for a new synagogue."

"You think our friend is playing both sides of the field."

"I haven't seen his opponent yet."

"Interesting."

"It's all interesting. That's part of the lure, isn't it? Everyone's heard of the Big D, but to meet him yourself, cut the deck and play cards for real stakes, is a chance that Mr. Average never gets. Even if you lose, or I should say 'when you lose,' because the deck is most definitely marked, it doesn't feel so bad. You're in good company, I mean bad company, I mean seriously interesting company."

"Sounds like you want me to join the game."

"I want you to win the game, Rabbi."

"How do I do that?"

"Up the ante, give him a glimpse of something he really wants, but can't get, nothing so cheap as a human soul, that's fodder for horses as far as he is concerned."

"So what is it that a creature like this requires?"

"If I knew what people wanted, I wouldn't have built this dog. I would've bought maybe a sneaker factory or a movie studio. All I'm saying is to trap the man with bait that he really wants; it's up to your finely honed intellect to determine what that is."

"In twenty-four hours."

"The fellow is nothing if not prompt."

"He was here at noon."

"Then he'll be back at noon."

THE RABBI did not sleep well that night. He considered the chips he could presumably toss onto the table. He could ante his percentage of the argyle works. That was the only item of value he had ever owned, except for his books. He was on the verge of a perception, and considered taking a nip to edge it into full consciousness, when the doorbell rang. Glimpsing a patch of uniform through the keyhole, Vandemeer was prepared to castigate his un-wanted guest for returning so early, but it was a messenger from an express delivery service.

The rabbi was not expecting anything, but he duly signed for the packet and opened it.

Tickets to the Netherlands fluttered out onto his desk. The Van-demeer sisters had received their brother's letter before it had been posted, but that was par for this new course, and of course they responded to its power with arms spread wide across the Atlantic. The tickets were first-class.

He stood up and allowed his eyes to roam the bookcases. He remembered the bookseller in rain-sodden Antwerp who sold him the curious volume on Maimonides. The man was distracted until money had exchanged hands, when he realized that he hadn't wanted to sell that particular volume. It was for display only, or his own personal reference. He tried to buy it back, offering twice the florins Vandemeer had just given him. The man was getting unpleas-ant, but a policeman wearing a black cloak was standing nearby smiling at the transaction. A deal was a deal.

Nevertheless, the bookseller wanted the volume back. That was why he had entered into this long-range plan, to send Eliezer a benefactor, poor Bensonbaum whose soul was to be had without even asking, in order to lure the rabbi to this place where the spring discharged its insidious thaw.

"Jews," the rabbi thought. If you want the buttonhook to go into the left side of the garment, you hold it inside out and start from the right. He opened the cracked leather binding and examined the marbelized frontispiece. Then he turned to the text. Where it had been difficult to comprehend the dense Gothic print, a dab of ink on the corner of a page elicited an instant grasp of the material. It was as if new lines were written over the old ones in a palimpsest of meaning. The book, newly interpreted by the wisdom of the bottle, was a demonic compendium, the Devil's own family Bible.

Every sentence had an opposite meaning once one had the wherewithal to perceive it. If God was singular, devils were multiple. If God was invisible, devils were all too palpable. Each one of Maimonides's thirteen principles of faith had its infernal counterpart. Finally, the student turned the last two pages which had stuck together centuries before. They came unglued and he read the line, "Property of Johannes Vandemeer."

Eliezer packed his bags as well as three apple-juice jugs of the sauce and took a limousine to the airport. His timing was impeccable. He waltzed through security, settled into the cushy seat he had been assigned, and the plane taxied down the runway. He didn't eat and didn't watch the movie, but sat under the cone of light from overhead, working. The rabbi wrote all night, scribbling to the rapid change in light as the 747 soared into the dawn.

A chauffeur picked Rabbi Vandemeer up at the airport and drove him through the elm-shaded drive to the family estate where Margaret, Eugenia, and Sue each lived with their husbands and children in vast American-style mansions that dwarfed the original homestead, which was kept as more of a museum than a residence. It was the common ground where they met to discuss business strategy.

The living room was paneled in chestnut, dotted with Rembrandt and Van Eyck drawings guarded by a sophisticated alarm system. In the place of honor centered on the carved stone mantle of an enormous fireplace stood a single ruby-tinged vial of the ambergris that represented the first Vandemeer's fortune, along with the one personal artifact of Johannes that had been passed down through the generations, his pipe.

Rabbi Vandemeer stood staring at the pipe and the rare emulsion that had lead him to this place hundreds of years after it had been siphoned from the belly of a dead whale when Margaret, the eldest, entered through the terrace, and greeted him, "From oil to oil. Your letter was enchanting."

Eliezer set the three jars of unholy pitch down on a long plank table that had been used to count the guilders that flooded Johannes's coffers. His descendants' use of the stuff would be shabby, no doubt similar to Irving's, something along the lines of a contract guaranteeing them better terms, or to bust the knitters' union at the factory. "The liquid is enchanting," he said. "I am merely enchanted."

"You were always subject to inspiration, dear Eliezer."

From the lips of the bitter matron whose nod could doom herds of shorn sheep to become mutton, as by-product, this was high praise. She was the most suspicious human being he had ever met, but now she believed. It was the power of the gift. Of course, she wanted it, because she had sensed the power in his letter. It was up to him to get something in return from her, and Eugenia and Sue.

The other two sisters entered now, wearing gowns in honor of this special visit, which presumably had the potential to thrust the family's domination of their chosen field into the next century. The shift from ambergris to argyle had been effected by Johannes's grandson in 1803 with the backing of a Rothschild cousin, whose own line still retained a silent percentage of the business along with Eliezer. The girls had long wished to rid themselves of these unwanted partners. Their vulgar merchants' souls understood nothing of magic.

"Let me tell you what I have in mind," Margaret said. They wished to put him in charge of sending their socks out to conquer the newly opening Soviet market. "With your powers of persuasion, we can sheathe two hundred million feet."

Eliezer replied, "I have never had and still have no interest in argyle. In fact, I wish to sell you my percentage of the business."

Eliezer retained a full fifteen percent of the argyle works, but he insisted that his receipts be deposited into a separate account he never touched except to buy books occasionally. His sisters knew that.

"What do you want?"

The shy, unworldly brother was no adept at strategy. All he could do was to lay his proposal on the pocked table. "A vial of ambergris and a pipe."

Margaret refused. She, who had not an ounce of sentiment, pretended to be offended. The vial was their history; it was a talisman, an heirloom.

Eliezer did not know if Margaret was acting on principle or negotiating. Assuming the latter, he increased the offer. "Along with all the profits that have been sitting in the bank for twenty years. Since my Bar Mitzvah."

Eugenia said coyly, "What about the land?"

"Of course."

Sue added, "The engravings, the silver, the linen, the mortgage-backed securities."

"Everything for the vial and the pipe."

Eliezer drove a hard bargain. He had nothing left to offer and they knew it. He gave them everything, but he would not leave without the ambergris and the pipe. The portrait of Johannes on the wall, commissioned from the school of Vermeer, frowned.

Another portrait beside that of the founder flattered the present generation, the sisters. It was commissioned of Arnold Mesches in the family tradition. Also of the family tradition, irrelevant parties such as Eliezer were deliberately left out of the frame.

The sisters agreed.

AN HOUR later, the rabbi was on the plane traveling westward, the precious satchel packed with the Vandemeer heirlooms tucked securely under his seat, Amsterdam to New York, New York to Hartford, and a taxi to Withers, just as his appointment came due.

"Boiler repair," the man grinned.

"Let's put that off just a bit."

"Good. What do you want?"

Vandemeer thought of his people's strivings. First he wanted to rewrite history, to bring back all of the martyrs of the ages. "Give me Spain and those who sank on the auto-da-fé."

"I told you, this is my century."

"Then give me Buchenwald. Give me the Gulag and the Israeli wrestling team from Munich."

"I can't change history. Those are the ground rules."

It had the ring of truth. That was why the Devil could not simply claim the book, but had to connive to obtain it.

"Then give me the future."

"You want the Messiah. I hate to tell you this, but He already came and I killed him. The *St. Louis*, that boat the United States refused to let dock, sent back to Germany, there was a white donkey in steerage. Besides, you've already got the Promised Land."

Eliezer laughed. He could have gone to Israel when he left the Netherlands, but he truly felt that the only home of the Jews was in the Diaspora. He saw his people as cosmopolitan wanderers, and was uneasy with the notion of the Jewish warrior. "That and a dollar gets me on the subway."

"You want money?"

The onetime heir to the argyle fortune scoffed, and the Devil knew better than to offer the other basic blandishments. The love of women was to be had if Eliezer turned his moony eyes upon the fair breed. What he wanted was wisdom, and with the assistance of the ink, he had that too. "First."

The Devil smiled, "I like a man who gets down to the nitty-gritty. Allow me to get my notebook, then you can shoot."

Rabbi Vandemeer did not comment on the ambiguity of the verb form. He had his own agenda. "Let Irving go."

"And in return . . ."

"In return, I will continue negotiations."

"That's nothing."

"That's all you have."

"Ridiculous, I utterly refuse," he sneered, as three Jeeps pulled into the parking lot, and men with unfurled blueprints began to point to the place where the sign for the new Hamilton Trust Company branch was to go.

"Thank you," Eliezer said.

"I don't get credit for that one. Irving has a good sense of demographics. Maybe the market's turning around."

Coincidence or face-saving pride, Rabbi Vandemeer agreed not to push his luck. "Next," he said.

"Oh, the synagogue. As soon as the bank comes in, I have a lovely old Victorian off the town square that will be made available. You may discover an unusual number of converts too. Judaism sweeps the Housatonic valley. A spiritual awakening, births, Bar Mitzvahs, funerals, an unending need for rabbinical advice."

"And a spring in the basement?"

"Goes without saying."

"Not so bad. Not really what I covet, but any rabbi must minister to his flock. There are worse ways of finding God."

"Hmph," the Devil snorted. "Enough?"

"Not quite, you see it's all fine and good if they find me, but what do I find?"

"What do you want?"

"I want what the Jewish people want. I want God to reveal himself in history."

"You want to meet the big fella?"

"Just for tea."

"Hey, He gets those requests all the time, that's what I'm here to take care of, the nuisances, the nudges, the ones who think that all the deity has to do is shine their shoes."

Rabbi Vandemeer looked down at his own dusty loafers. He was exempt from the lures of pride. "Just for tea—there's a few questions I'd like to ask."

"Can't do it."

"But . . ."

"Look, I've got a lot of ability, but only so much. I've got a few questions I'd like to ask myself."

Rabbi Vandemeer peered at his visitor and he realized that the Devil wanted the same thing he did, proof of God's presence and a justification of His ways to man. But just as the miraculous change in Vandemeer was proof of the Devil's existence, wasn't the fiend himself proof of an opposing force?

Again, the Evil One read his antagonist's mind. "It's like a mathematical equation that comes to infinity. You believe the sideways eight symbol, but do you understand it?"

For the first time, the rabbi did understand the Devil's purpose. Satan, more desperately than any of his victims, needed to know that there was a God. "Who are you?" Vandemeer demanded.

"I am that I am." It was God's words to Moses out of the burning bush, but it was pure bravado, wishful thinking by a little boy from Strasbourg who snuck onto the deity's throne, hoping against hope that his heresy would compel refutation from a silent master. "And your time is just about up. I've got a schoolteacher in Milwaukee who wants to meet little boys."

The Devil was getting tough. He gestured to the black lake in which they stood, and it began to funnel down into the drain.

"You want the book?"

"Yes."

"I'll give it to you, in return for one more thing."

"What's that?"

"A light."

"You mean spiritual illumination."

"No, I mean a match."

"A match?"

"Stick or paper, makes no difference. I don't usually smoke, but in honor of the occasion, I've broken out the patriarch's pipe." Rabbi Vandemeer began to tamp tobacco from a pouch into the bowl.

The Devil did not know what to make of this request, but when Eliezer nonchalantly handed him the volume in which the Devil had sought to find his own version of illumination, he snapped his fingers and a flame spurted from the nails.

Rabbi Vandemeer cupped his palm about the hand and inhaled deeply. He exhaled a plume of smoke and Satan coughed.

Eliezer thought of the whale oil that founded the family fortune. Wasn't he a whale on the shore of the new world, gasping for breath? Wasn't the religion of the sages a whale that could not swim in the thinner spirit of modernity? Wasn't the Devil a whale-size figure without potency here in the society of cheap celebrity? Where was the faith both of them sought if not in the picayune details of daily life? Better to be an honest herring than a bogus leviathan.

The rabbi scorned the visions of grandeur the Devil dangled before him. It was no wonder that the greatest evils of the century began with a notion of the ideal, and that was why they had appealed to so many people. Wasn't this proof that the ideal was the danger? Should he seek the basics, instead, maybe turn back to the argyle works to make socks for the masses?

All Eliezer really wanted from Heaven was to ease the pain of his toes, but if it was necessary to limp through what Satan called his "pallid simulacrum of life," so be it.

It was time to reclaim his humanity. Eliezer kissed good-bye the infinite possibilities offered by the substance of perfection. He threw the vial of ambergris to the floor, and the ruby shards exploded to the four corners. The smelly waxy matter spread more slowly, encasing the Devil's cloven, argyle-covered hooves, and Eliezer dumped the burning clot of tobacco from Johannes's pipe to the floor.

Unlike the God who spoke to Moses, the Devil was consumable. He disappeared in an oily plume that left a smudge on the ceiling.

Rabbi Vandemeer emerged from the ashes, triumphant, ineloquent, mortal.

Old Words for New

SLUMPED OVER the tablets, in dun khakis and pith helmet,
Professor Phragus resembled a sand dune. His head rested on one flat
palm while his other hand traced idly over the patterns engraved
beneath him. His eyes, irritated by the sweat and the dust, were
closed, but he still recognized the shapes under his fingers, like a
blind man reading Braille. He knew the birds and the snakes, the
balances and the thrones, a mile of horses, and the different stick
men, standing, running, bowing. Most of all he knew and let his
fingers linger on the one strange figure he could not define. It was a
derangement of intersecting lines, arcs, and angles, and it was repeated at vital junctures of the text in its identical, incomprehensible form. The professor stirred. Even the clarity of the horses and
balances was rendered suspect by the mystery the extraordinary figure (a lightning storm?) engendered. The professor was like a blind
man who can suddenly see, but still cannot understand.

Day after day, Professor Phragus returned to the small whitewashed room overlooking the dig. First he would skim whatever had
been unearthed the previous day, but the bones and pottery did not
interest him. "Trinkets. If I had my way I'd bury them again," he

muttered, shocking both students and colleagues. He let the artifacts sift through his fingers like the sand that was sifted to find them. When done with his disagreeable duty, he could stand, listing to the right like an ill-laden skiff, alone with the slowly emerging city of the past.

The view was quite different from the one onto campus from Hamilton Hall, but even if several continents and several thousand years separated the two, the one had become the other. It was the professor's chosen mission to ascertain how the change, more wonderful, more inevitable than that from chrysalis to Monarch, came about.

He turned his broad shoulders and enormous paunch away from the sunburned landscape to the prefabricated Quonset hut like a burial mound that served as his home away from academia. There he descended into the crypt of the lost civilization to enter into communion with it through the three tablets and 116 fragments in which it spoke. He forgot the ceramic jars and lapis lazuli jewelry and the mottled, neolithic skulls: Words were the treasure, language the key. So he sat by the tablets, looking, thinking, touching. By his side, a pen and paper rested should he wish to take notes, but the paper remained blank and the ink dried in the pen. Were the birds symbols for gods or were they merely crows? Did the balances measure wheat, gold, or justice? Most of all, what was the last, strange, frenzied configuration? A tidal wave?

The tablets were a foot wide and three feet long and two inches thick. Droplets of the professor's sweat were the first moisture they had felt in millennia. They were made of reddish-beige baked mud brick, and their texture was rough, but their reliefs were as clear as the letters on a page. There were animals and objects, glossed by an abstract chicken-scratched alphabet. Decoding, however, was not the final step. From mathematical principles of frequency and juxtaposition, one could work from letters to words, but from words to meaning was a larger task. Such a wealth of obscure mythopoetical significance was attached to each term that no amount of sheer diligence could overleap it.

As inspiration had written, so could only inspiration comprehend. That was why Professor Theodore Aloysius Phragus (B.A., London, 1923; M.A., London, 1924; Ph.D., Oxford, 1928; Curator, British Museum, 1929–1939; Major, African Staff, His Majesty's Armed Forces, 1939–1943; Colonel, Cyphers, 1943–1945; Associate Professor, University of Damascus, 1946–1950; Professor, Columbia University, New York, 1950–1954, 1956–present; Drinan Visiting Professor, Harvard University, Massachusetts, 1955; Honorary Degrees: Harvard, London, Amherst; author of *Totemism in the Ancient Near East* (1924); *Signs, Symbols, and Sentences* (1931); *The Devotion of the Ox* (1932); *Modes of Thought*, Volume One, *Oral* (1935); Volume Two, *Written* (1938); *The Phrases of the Moon* (1949); *Modes of Thought*, Volume Three, *Silent* (1956); never married; no children; called "Froggie" behind his back) was back in the Mideast, drinking bottled water and sweating it out, and happier than he had been in years.

There was a rap on the door, but the professor ignored it. He brushed a few long hairs off his forehead and when the sound repeated itself he growled, "Come in already before you knock the damn thing down."

It was Morraine, of course. No one else would dare to disturb Phragus. Complete privacy was one of the conditions he laid down before agreeing to join the expedition, but as head of the expedition Morraine felt himself exempt from this rule and insisted that the professor go through a daily charade of good fellowship. "I came to see what I could do for you," Morraine said, sitting gracefully on the edge of the table, smiling at the grimace the professor could not contain when anyone else neared "his" tablets.

"Nothing."

"New shards," Morraine informed him. Despite the pointed lack of response, he went on. "One jar almost intact. Fantastic glaze. Museum quality."

"If I want museum quality, I will go to the museum."

"Now you're being funny."

The professor stood up, and the two faced each other over the table that brought them together. The bulk of the one and the wiry intensity of the other, they were like elephant and leopard, natural enemies.

Until the tablets were found, Phragus had not been particularly interested in the Nastrokhan dig. He was aware of it, as he was of every spade that broke the brittle Mideast ground. He had followed Morraine's progress in the professional journals, and one day he had been mildly surprised to find a feature in the *Times*. Morraine belonged to the new generation of archaeological researchers who needed publicity to justify their funding. Gone were the days when the great institutions would send people out for a decade on a hunch. But Morraine did not merely tolerate this state of affairs; he thrived on it. Nevertheless, he lacked the respectability that a name like Theodore Aloysius Phragus could grant him. Unsolicited, he sent to Hamilton Hall a catalogue of everything found, the pottery, the jewelry, the bones. What interested Phragus, however, was what wasn't cited—weapons. No knives, no clubs, no battle-axes. He sent a short note halfway around the world to this effect.

After this one brief exchange, the professor was subsequently mentioned by the *Times* as a sponsor of the Nastrokhan expedition. Livid, he was about to issue a denial when a single grainy photograph of the first tablet came through the post. With uncharacteristic understatement, all Morraine wrote was, "Thought this might be up your alley."

Phragus pushed his heavy black-rimmed glasses onto the bridge of his doughy nose. Although it was noon, he turned on the overhead light in his office and then focused the desk lamp until it was as bright four stories above College Walk as it was in Nastrokhan. An hour later, he stood with elderly vanity in front of a mirror, his old pith helmet at a rakish slant.

"Too bad we can't dig on Fifth Avenue, hey?"

Phragus was jolted from his reverie. He was susceptible to a pleasant entrancement in the desert, the light making for distraction, the heat for indolence, the vistas taking his thoughts to them. Why not Fifth Avenue? Couldn't Phragus have studied enormous blowups of the photographs in New York? Wouldn't Morraine have shipped the tablets themselves to New York? What a world-hungry man like Morraine could never understand was that the desert was what the tablets had emerged from, returned to, and been discovered in, and that it was the only place they could ever be understood.

"Well, if you're not interested," Morraine said, and started toward the door. The words drifting behind him like smoke, he continued, "It's just that this jar has the same pattern as your tablets do and I thought that—"

"What?"

"Yes, the strange one, the one you can't make out. Only here it's continuous, clear around the jug."

"C'mon, man, by all means let's see it. Where? Where?" and the professor limped along as eager as a child while Morraine led the way.

Stroke angling up through curves drifting down, overlapping, intersecting, there the figure was. The professor circled it with fascination and reverence. He saw the undrawn line where it could be split and pressed into the two-dimensional shape he thought he knew so well. How could he have missed the fact that the left edge fit the right perfectly, and what did this mean? Was it a seamless web that signified nothing, or maybe Nothing, the original cypher from which substance emanated? No, the idea of the void occurred to him simply because his own mind was blank. The shape had become Phragus's personal Rorschach blot. As he had by turns felt baffled or frustrated, he read it as a symbol of chaos or failure. To construe the blot's objective truth the professor would have to immerse himself in the world which produced it. He was certain that as language would prove the key to the world his students were literally unearthing, the blot was the key to the language.

"I've been wondering if we've been dealing with an outpost of the Assyrian Empire," Morraine suggested.

"I doubt it," Phragus harrumphed. As he was humble before the dead, he was gruff to the living.

"The dates are right. The location is right. Even something in the look of the language is right."

"I think you should leave the language to me."

"I think I have a certain knowledge too."

"And how do you reconcile the lack of weapons with the notoriously warlike nature of the mother country?"

"I have a theory."

"Do enlighten me."

Claude Morraine (B.A., Université Lyonnaise, 1958; M.A., Sorbonne, 1960; Teacher, École de San Rudolfo, Zurich, 1961–1963; Junior Attaché, French Embassy, Istanbul, 1965–1967; Ph.D., American University in Rome, 1969; Associate Professor, American University in Rome, 1970–1972, 1974–present; Visiting Professor, New York University, 1973; author of A Quilted Civilization (1970); married Cynthia von Kirsten; divorced; no children) was as dark as an Assyrian. He would have looked good in a camel-skin tunic with a bronze helmet with purple feathers and a twin-bladed hatchet. He said: "The belief in life after death is common throughout the Fertile Crescent. That's why food is left in tombs, to help the departed cope with the rigors of the hereafter. But what if these people were so suspicious that they feared their own ancestors? If the dead could use food, why not arms? If they could influence life spiritually, why not materially? Better to forbid them weapons."

"Ingenious, but wrong. The dead may be feared, but they are also respected. If they did not take weapons to their beyond, they did not use them in Nastrokhan. I'm beginning to think that we may have chanced upon genuine pacifists here."

"Which may explain why they died out so abruptly." Morraine carelessly picked up the jar.

"You . . ."

Morraine continued, "Granted, some symbols, like your favorite, are not typically Assyrian, but I suggest that this was caused by the fragmentation of the culture at a later date. I would also suggest that what we have in Nastrokhan may be an extreme case of Assyrianism, the pupil outdoing the master as it were."

"A phenomenon you no doubt think yourself familiar with."

"Stranger things have happened." Morraine balanced the jar on the tip of his forefinger. Then he spun it like a top.

The design blurred, yet Phragus felt himself able to follow its successive revolutions. There was something about its circularity that he could not resist, but this was weakness. The circularity was superfluous. On clay, as writing, the pattern had meaning; on a jar that probably held fermented grains it did not. "Ornamentation," the professor snorted.

"Museum quality."

The professor wanted to return to his hermit's retreat, but his concentration was gone. He wandered out into the excavations.

The sun was high and the only shadows were at the bottoms of the trenches. Sand crumbled in as the professor stood too close to the edge, as he had thirty years before, when he found his limp. It had been night, far south of Nastrokhan, in a moon-worshiping culture whose central code could not be cracked. The young Phragus wished to see the fullness for himself with the eyes of the dead. Gazing up, he had slipped into an open pit. His bone snapped like a finger with satisfaction. The text in question was equivalent to the lunar cycle, but its sections had to be emphasized according to the phase. The same word had opposite meanings at the beginning and end of the text. He was discovered the next morning, lying like a corpse in an unfilled grave, his leg swollen beyond any future repair, the cult revealed. Thirty years later, he still strode heedlessly over the trenches, thrusting his bulk forward, drawing his bad leg behind him.

Blue-jeaned students shaded their eyes with hands holding the picks they used to pry relics from the earth's tenacious grip. They had not seen Froggie before, but when they returned to their universities in the autumn they would say that they worked with him.

Foundations were being uncovered all about him as the ancient city rose from the desert. There were enormous truncated pillars, half-walls with traces of mosaics which would, the professor was certain, expose that same unknown pattern flamboyantly. It was something of such magnitude as to be worthy of worship as a manifestation of the Ultimate—but what? An earthquake?

The professor remembered his first trip to the Mideast. Without oil wealth, Teheran and Bagdad were not much different from Nastrokhan. The cradle of civilization was an eerie, forgotten part of the modern world, but T. A. Phragus adapted well. His body grew heavier to hold water like a camel, and his naturally ruddy complexion grew redder than ever as he hunted for invisible cities. Some were found through a practiced reading of the topography, but others were discovered from sheer intuition. As if seeking water, Phragus and his breed roamed the wasteland with psychic dowsing rods, which jerked down God knew where God knew why. Damned if they didn't strike more often than not.

Phragus knew the cities he discovered in a way he could never know London or New York. Take a street, for example, any ancient street. Its width told him about the forms of transportation, foot, mule, or cart, and about the economy, subsistence, or market, and about the society. Then there was the jewelry and the pottery and the bones, invaluable storehouses of information. But mostly it was through the tongue that the professor acquainted himself with the primitive mind. Here man was still the measure of all things, except the one thing he chose to worship, and that varied from culture to culture—the Persians with their laws, the Assyrians with their weapons, the Eblans with their books. It was an intellectual game: Find the unifying element and you could grasp the internal logic of a vanished civilization.

Phragus absentmindedly crossed the trenches and climbed the broken steps onto the flat expanse of a ruined temple. Suddenly, it occurred to him that the holy place was not bereft of statues, plundered by centuries of thieves, as he had assumed, but that it had never boasted such frivolity. He felt as if he were on the verge of revelation, but it was elusive. He peered across the manmade plateau to the sand which had once been sand-colored grain. Under cultivation, the arid soil was transformed into healthy red mud. Dried and imprinted, it bridged the ages to speak to Theodore Aloysius Phragus as if written especially for him.

Individual rays of light danced on the temple grounds. The professor watched them curiously. They appeared to separate and then to rejoin into stick-figure men, walking, running, bowing beside horses, birds, and balances. Emerging from between their slit mouths like a comic balloon was the familiar indecipherable pattern.

"What is this?" Phragus demanded. "Tell me what you fear and love. Is it earth, air, water, flame?"

The necropolis was silent. Its concerns were not of this world. Its symbol was meant to be incomprehensible because it symbolized the ineffable, without need for weaponry to protect its divinity. Rather than a manifestation of the power, it was Power itself. Phragus fell to his knees. Here, millennia before Moses or Mohammed, was the archaeological find of the century, the birthplace of the single, eternal, monotheistic God.

INTERLOGUE FROM the curriculum of the Sabbio School of Ancient Affairs:

> Only one people went against the common current of violent inter-action. The Nassyrians, so named by their discoverers, Drs. Claude Morraine and Theodore A. Phragus, after the present-day village of Nastrokhan and the historically Assyrian territory, were the forerun-ners of all humanistic philosophies. The Nassyrians bore no weapons and knew no evil. Their concerns were of God, as we know from the few clay tablets which survived their authors. It has been conjectured that theirs was the original Eden prior to their obliteration by enemies circa 1900 B.C.

PROFESSOR EMERITUS Theodore Aloysius Phragus sat at his desk like a pyramid. Sedentariness had bred fat and he positively overflowed his chair. His eyes were closed, but he saw snakes and horses on the insides of his puffy lids, and balances and thrones and, hovering benignly above all, the figure of God.

On the reissue of the monumental trilogy, *The Modes of Thought*, Professor Phragus dismissed it. "Bunk. Rubbish. Useless lists of the dead," he wrote to his publishers, who wisely decided to omit his comments from the dust jacket. He began a second trilogy. *The Modes of Action*. Volume One, *Peace*, 1977, took its primary cue from the Nassyrian culture he had defined, but even this was too academic for his recently awakened soul. Volume Two, *Conflict*,

1979, was a lament that briefly attained best-seller status because of its bloodier descriptive passages ranging from Thermopylae to Stalingrad. But Phragus hardly noticed his season of fame. He pondered Volume Three, the untitled utopian synthesis of his labors. Here he wished to put forth no less than a blueprint for a perfect world and to spur his readers to build it. Modern society was rushing pell-mell to oblivion, yet not even his fellow archaeologists could see past the residuum they dug up to the salvation vouchsafed them. It was vital to heed the lesson of Nastrokhan, but as inspiration had written, so could only inspiration rewrite. So the professor sat with the treasure locked inside of him, thinking. By his side, a typewriter and paper rested should he wish to take advantage, but the paper remained blank and the typewriter quiet.

Day after day, Phragus returned to his cluttered office overlooking College Walk. First he graded his students' theses. Then he skimmed the professional journals, whose covers he barely restrained himself from slashing with his red pencil, "Pedantic drivel." He stood, tilting even more to the right now, due to a phlebitis which cost him his bad limb. Grinning at misfortune, he said, "Not to worry. They'll give me a peg and I'll change my name to Ahab, except I look more like the whale." Just because his body had failed him didn't mean that he was going to roll over and dedicate his creaky bones to whatever future archaeologist was bound to retrieve them from the ruins of technological society. He looked down. It was a very different view from the one onto the dig at Nastrokhan, but even if several continents and several thousand years separated the two, the one had emerged from the other. It was the professor's newly chosen mission to discover how such a noble lineage could produce such a despicable offspring. He gazed up at the large photograph of the tablets that had enlightened him and a sense of well-being coursed through him.

Then there was a knock on the door. It was a sharp, peremptory rap, not the timorous *tick tick* of students, the inquisitive *knahhck* of pilgrims, the healthy *cathump* of friends. Phragus knew that rap, but from where and when he wasn't certain.

The knock repeated itself, and it was this arrogant insistence more than the particular sound that jogged his memory. "Come in," he said.

Morraine's face was older, but the distinctively youthful look of intensive thought misapplied could not be masked. Phragus was nonetheless grateful to the man through whom he had discovered his own life's work. "Hello, Claude. How can I help you?"

"As always, I came to see if I could help you, Professor."

Maybe it was Phragus's imagination, but he thought that even this polite greeting was accented with derision.

Morraine meanwhile gestured to the blowup of the original tablet. "That was a long time ago," he said. "Things have changed."

"For the better."

"For me. . . . You stayed in the desert."

"Yes, I was interested. And you?"

"I took the opportunity to come to Fifth Avenue."

Phragus grunted. The mere appearance of this man sapped the magic from life. Worse, the attitude was contagious. The professor sneered, "So what are you doing so far uptown? Aren't you afraid you'll get the bends?"

"New discovery."

Phragus had all the discoveries he needed. He allowed his eyes to rest on the perfect cosmological symbol on the wall.

"Well, if you're not interested," Morraine said, letting his words drift out in the insinuating tone that turned everything into conspiracy. "It's just that there's that same symbol of yours, the one you call God, and it's appeared in a new aspect."

This time, however, Morraine could not pique the professor. It was no longer the setting of the symbol that mattered. It was not even the symbol itself, but the reality it stood for. "It may appear in any aspect. It is everywhere."

"Don't tell me you're getting mystical, Professor. I can't believe you're not interested in this."

"Of course, I am interested in any manifestation of the One. But it is the future presence of the redemptive spirit—"

"Shut up," Morraine snapped. The scent of sanctity irked him. "This isn't a social call. You are the one person who is as involved with it as I am, and I am the one person who has as much to lose as you do."

"Lose?"

"I'm not going to play the hypocritical admirer like all the others who fawn at your pudgy feet. . . ."

"Foot," the professor blandly corrected him.

"Eh?"

"Foot. Singular. I have only one foot." He wagged his stump, feeling a queer satisfaction with the abuse he was bearing.

Morraine was equally pleased to vent the abuse. Three days and precious little sleep ago, he had flown out to the desert in order to retrieve personally the object that sat in his jacket pocket. He had spent the entire return flight in horrified contemplation of the meaning of the object and had reluctantly decided that Phragus was the only one to whom he could confide. He had come to the university straight from the airport. "I don't care if you have one nostril and three eyes. *We* have a problem, and *we* have to deal with it."

The professor sat with his hands clasped prayerfully in front of him. He peered down at the table where Morraine had thrown something long and thin and wrapped in tissue paper. Phragus disunited his fingers and slowly unwrapped the object. He was absurdly careful not to rip the green paper. Then he saw it, first the symbol composed of lines, arc, and angles engraved on a handle of sorts. Then he saw the object itself. It was a knife. It burned Phragus's palm like a brand. "A forgery?"

Morraine laughed contemptuously. "You think I would be here if it was a fraud? I tried every test from Carbon 14 to Visiger Analysis. They all check out."

Phragus could not believe it.

Morraine went on. "It was found in the extended Nastrokhani digs, miles from where we left off. A weapon! What do you think it was used for, carving apples in the garden of Eden? A weapon for God's sake. Do you know what that means, you bloated old fool?"

Phragus turned to him with impassive generosity. "I'm sure that I can imagine what it was used for."

"Damn right. And whether it was battle or, heaven forbid, sacrifice, either way it blows our theories and reputations to shreds. Just one big hot air–filled balloon and this." He picked the object up, heedless of its immeasurable value, and thrust it down into the professor's desk. "Pop."

The knife vibrated, the symbol a blur until the professor extended a single fat finger to steady it. He felt dizzy. He didn't care about his reputation, but how could a weapon fit into the perfect pacifist society? There wasn't even a word for knife or dagger in the Nassyrian language. Phragus had worked for months outward from the symbol for God to create the godly tongue. "Perhaps knives were an unfortunate necessity considered unworthy of language," he mused. "Just as God did not exist until the Nassyrians created Him by their symbol, so the weapon did not exist, because they refused to grant it the recognition of its own symbol."

"Nonsense," Morraine retorted. "People just don't work that way. They name what they use. They use what they need. They need what they name."

"No, no," the professor became agitated. He felt Volume Three of his opus taking shape. "No, you don't understand. This is the key I've been waiting for. The secret is not only the creation of good, but the negation of evil. As a species, we've made the primary mistake of giving names to weapons and money and cancer. By naming these things we've surrendered to their reality. If we can reverse the process, we can compel life to confirm our ideals. If we eliminate certain words from our vocabulary, the concepts they represent will cease to exist."

As the old professor's eyes misted, Morraine realized that he would get no further aid from this quarter. Without bothering to say "Adieu," he yanked the knife from the desk and strode to the door and exited, but Theodore Aloysius Phragus didn't notice. Claude Morraine and his knife no longer existed for him.

DESPITE THE professor's willful blindness, Claude Morraine sat in his study on the twenty-third floor of a modern apartment tower and contemplated the lights of the city beneath him. It was the neon and chrome of the twentieth century A.D. that made his blood quicken. He had grown accustomed to the good life, and it was all in jeopardy now because of a reckless judgment of a decade ago. He did not pause to reflect that his name had been made precisely because of that judgment. He sat with a brandy in one hand, the other absentmindedly stroking his cat, Xerxes.

He wracked his brain to find a way to shut down the excavation, to no effect. It was only because he was an honorary director that the acting director thought it fit to give him first crack at the new find. But nobody had the power to pick up the two hundred eager-beaver students toiling under the sun, now that the dig was more fertile than at any time since the halcyon days of the venerable Froggie.

Neither could the evidence be suppressed. There were no articles yet, but word was leaking. Imagine a tear of oil dropped into a barrel of rainwater. Take a drink. The one part per million contaminant cannot possibly be discerned, yet the knowledge of the taint will be enough to impart a taste.

He had to come up with an explanation for the impossible weapon. Another culture stealing Nassyrian symbology? A later era? Synchroneity? No, intellectual lances would gleefully pierce these balloons as easily as they would the old lunatic's lingorealism. Imagine, believing he could create the truth.

And then it hit him—the truth. Not the old man's truth, but the real thing. Sometimes Claude was too devious for his own good. He was not afraid of being proven wrong, but of someone else finding the proof. He could forestall this simply by doing the work himself. By exploding his own theory, he would show, if anything, his own indefatigable pursuit of wisdom. And he had a great advantage. He was in sole possession of the evidence.

Like Phragus, Morraine knew that language was the key to the puzzle. As the elder had noted, there was no word for knife, or was there? Could the explanation be as elementary as a single word's mistranslation? No, there was a larger error here. It was a paradox to picture a saint wielding a knife. Phragus had made Nassyrian holiness so real that it took Morraine a moment to realize that there was nothing but Phragus's words to verify that repulsive piety. Since the knife most definitely existed, could it be possible that the saint did not? He began to smile.

Claude Morraine, in navy silk suit, allowed his own vision of the Nassyrian man to emerge, riding out of the dunes in armor, greaves and guards, and plumed helmets, which he suddenly knew with utter certainty would be uncovered in further excavations. All historical thought until now showed that ancient man's was a brutal life. Struggle was the ultimate truth here. More than struggle, conflict. More than conflict.

Damn that old man! How had Morraine let himself in for that fuzzy-minded, wishful-thinking pap? As late in the game as 3:00 P.M. today he had wanted to shift Phragus's emphasis to accommodate the knife, but now that he knew the meaning of the symbol on the knife's handle he also knew that it was not Phragus's emphasis that was wrong, but his entire concept. The Nassyrian civilization's primary value and ultimate goal, stated and exalted by the mystical symbol, was not God, but War.

INTERLOGUE FROM the 73rd Annual Symposium of the Union of PreHebrew Philologists:

> In one of the most dramatic reversals in modern intellectual history, the language of the Nassyrian people has been determined to proceed from a warriorlike disposition diametrically opposed to the peace-loving family man produced by their first translator, T. A. Phragus. Rather than the moral culture destroyed by the violent Assyrians, they were the final efflorescence of Assyrianism. This new outlook is described by Claude Morraine in his book, *Stab in the Heart*, 1980. Professor Morraine also describes the process by which a fallacy came to dominate the usually cautious archaeological community.

PROFESSOR PHRAGUS'S studies ranged yet farther afield, from the desert to the stars to encompass flying saucers and superior intelligences. The results, no longer welcome in the professional journals of his trade, were published in magazines with lurid covers.

Phragus continued to lecture on "the virtuous nature of the pre-Christian commune," but his classes were progressively undersubscribed, requiring a shift from the mahogany-panelled auditorium on the ground floor of Hamilton Hall to a drafty box next to the fourth-floor men's room. He arrived late and left early, and his discourse tended to wander as his connections with the physical world became ever more tenuous. He even lost weight, through lack of interest in food rather than any active concern for his health.

Finally, the head of his department managed to bump discreetly into his once-prized eminence one autumn day after dark when the last sophomore had left for the local pub. The professor remained at his desk, tossing obscurely marked sticks. "Working late, Theodore?"

"Yes," the professor muttered, scribbling notes in a cramped script on a yellow legal pad. "Look," he said, throwing the sticks three times to the same pattern. "What do you think that means?"

"Theodore, have you considered taking a sabbatical lately? I know that you're not due for another two years, but we could stretch the rules. . . ."

Phragus looked up, paused, and accepted the proffered gift, much to the relief of the dean, who was glad to bribe him to avoid the embarrassment of his presence. Both tacitly assumed that the discredited academic would announce his retirement after his vacation.

At ease now, the head of the department grew conversational. "Where do you think you'll go, Theodore?" he asked, assuming London.

"There's only one place I can go."

The bureaucrat understood. "Do you think that's advisable?"

"It's necessary."

But even as T. A. Phragus alit from the dusty Mercedes taxi that had driven him from the capital, he began to have doubts.

The grimace on the bland face of the acting director of the Nastrokhani expedition was not reassuring. Neither was the most curious fact that the man's linens were sweat-free, his trousers pressed. Samuel Salem (B.A., Harvard, Massachusetts, 1953; M.A., Harvard, 1955; Associate Curator, Salem Collection, Boston Museum of Antiquities, 1956–1958; Pederson Chair, University of Massachusetts, 1969–1972; Co-Sponsor of the Morraine Chair at the Boston Museum of Antiquities; married Valeria Pederson Salem; no children) asked, "How can I help you?"

"I came to see if I could help you," the professor answered, frightening his host.

Salem gestured. "As you can see, we've come a long way." The excavations stretched to the horizon. More importantly, the headquarters were now air-conditioned.

Phragus preferred the hot sun and the grit in his pores. "I won't be any bother."

A cluster of student volunteers had gathered behind Mr. Salem to ogle the visitor. One of them said to another, "No bother? Do you know how hard I studied Nassyrian? Got an 'A' too. Came here and it's upside down."

His companion whispered, "If you can't believe what the teachers say, what can you believe?"

Froggie's ears were keener than the youth might have expected. He turned and answered the lad's rhetorical question with a definitive, "Truth."

The boy seemed to wither, but Mr. Salem mildly dug, "A subject of great conjecture."

The professor tipped an imaginary hat. But the coolness of his ostensible peer and the disrespect of the students were insignificant compared to the worrisome voices of the past. Nastrokhan itself was different from what it had been. Mr. Salem was correct; the city had grown enormously. The farthest boundaries of Phragus's day, referred to as the "old town," occupied a corner of the immense compound. It was surrounded by a web of "new town" whose avenues bespoke commerce and sophistication. A Russian observer reminded of Red Square was moved to write a monograph on the military parades that must have passed by in rows of horses with lines of men. Even the contemporary traffic was great. Jeeps crisscrossed the intersections, bearing students back and forth from their lodgings to the digs. Off to the east, a film crew was erecting a scaffold to produce a deodorant commercial while a busload of tourists was disembarking with cameras hanging about their necks like amulets.

Professor Phragus chose to follow the tourists, who tramped after a tall guide in a baseball cap. The professor was curious to hear what the man had to say, but he was too far away to distinguish anything but the babble of successive English, French, and German narrations. Then the diverse group raised their cameras as one, and the professor moved in to see what they were photographing with such diligent universality.

It was an idol of vaguely humanoid features, two eyes, a nose, and an open mouth. Extending sideways from its trunk, however, were claws instead of arms, clutching a knife and a twin-bladed axe. On the idol's forehead was the omnipresent symbol in which the professor had once discerned God.

Struck, as if on his own forehead, Phragus staggered back and let the group advance without him. He could tolerate, nay, thrive on the obloquy of humanity, but the betrayal of his Lord was too great a blow for him to sustain. Instead of the comfort he needed, Nastrokhan had confirmed his worst fears.

He rushed down the nearest roadway until he came upon a mass of students eagerly uncovering a communal burial mound, gloating over the charred bones that were the sole recollection of the massacres of yore. He veered, but was promptly brought up against the grandiose arsenal in which a myriad of weaponry was stored. The city of warriors surrounded him.

He began to avoid the main roads, to take at each intersection the path of greater resistance, the narrower the better. Though it was difficult for the one-legged scholar to climb the heaps of bricks and fallen pillars, he did. Wending away from people, he squeezed his bulk between walls barely a foot apart, into the impoverished regions of the old town he loved. Here, he sought out the original temple in which he had been granted his bogus revelation. After a dozen dead ends, he slipped through one final crevice and found himself on the familiar sacred ground.

The stone was the same veiny gray as the sky, and the uniformity of the surfaces made him feel as if he were inside an egg. He stumped about there, on the vacant plateau, bereaved by the end of his best brainchild. How could he be so deluded as to expect to find a more perfect world here? The temple's signal purity was evidently the result of its poor congregation's inability to raise the funds to purchase an idol. He felt that the ruins about him were the ruins of his own life.

But as his metal-tipped crutch beat an uneven rhythm on the temple's stone floor, he became aware of something odd. Everytime he crossed one particular block, where the diagonals from the corners met, the tone of the tap changed. He performed a series of exploratory taps to verify this. On every side of the particular square which measured perhaps a meter across, the ground gave solid thumps, but the one spot was different. He bent down and began picking at the dirt between the enormous slabs. Suddenly the stone in question swung away on a hinge like a gallows' trapdoor. Underneath, there was a stairway with a million motes of dust hovering in the shaft. The professor glanced involuntarily around him, like a little boy who has broken his mother's favorite vase. He bent low to peer down the staircase, but he could not see past the dust and the dense crosshatching of thousands of years of spiders' webs. He brushed at the webs with his free arm and then he stepped onto the first of the rough stairs.

There were only five steps, so that he had to stoop when he arrived at the base. Using his crutch now like a blind man a cane, he tapped forward into the shadows. He could have sworn that he and Claude Morraine had done core samples to determine whether the temple was built upon the remains of an earlier culture. Maybe there had been traces of a primitive campfire, but surely no rooms of this extent. Perhaps it was this awareness that made Phragus preter-naturally sensitive, but when a figure suddenly loomed out of the recesses, the professor gasped and raised his crutch in defense. But he lost his balance and toppled back, and the impression of floating was the last thing he noticed before his head smashed into the hard rock wall.

When he woke, the vault was dimly lit by an unidentifiable source. There was a rude wooden table, its legs carved from solid cedar, the pieces fit together without nails. Was this an indication of craft or merely a sign of the lack of metallurgy? Three men in roughly woven cloth sat at the table, their heads bent, conferring in a low murmur. One of them was hunched with age, his white hair straggling past a wrinkled neck. Another was upright, his profile sharp. The third was obscured by the first two.

Professor Phragus's first thought was that these were native por-ters who used this secret chamber to slack off and play cards. His body numbed by concussion, the professor concentrated on the few words that came to him, a native dialect no doubt. But there was something about the repetition of sounds that stirred him. Each idiom has a distinctive pattern, and the pattern here was ancient. In the terminology used to describe certain languages, it was dead.

Yet it was familiar.

The youngest man at the table shifted position and, in the gap between him and the old man, Professor Phragus could see the third man, his chest bright with rudimentary pigment daubed on in a derangement of intersecting lines, arcs, and angles.

It struck the professor that the men were speaking in the same pattern as the symbols of the famous Nassyrian text. Though he had translated it, or thought he had, he had no idea what it sounded like. The vowels, it seemed, were clear, the consonants smooth. It took another minute for him to comprehend the speaker's meaning.

The young man spoke with a tenseness that belied his tongue's natural lilt. He said, "We should kill him." The literal meaning was, "We should cease his being," but Phragus understood.

The elder responded with a word that was used frequently in the original tablets. "Why?" The answer was usually the central figure that Phragus had taken so long to mistake.

"He is a danger."

"He is a stranger."

"He is from the outside, and we must take his existence from him."

The elderly man put his hands to his ears as if he were in great pain.

The younger persisted. "You cannot protect yourself from my thoughts."

Professor Phragus listened to the men argue over his fate with an eerie calm.

The elder seemed to want to fold into the table, while the younger stood, and then, at a loss for words, slapped at the pathetically exposed dome of the elder's head. There was a hush.

Then the third man, a kind of judge, spoke to the youth. "You have violated our most basic precepts. You have lifted arm against your fellow. Worse, you have attempted to distort our language in a way that I cannot understand. You have tried to falsify it with your ideas. This we cannot abide. You no longer have being."

At first, the professor was shocked at the severity of the judgment. But it further transpired that the beneficence of the two peaceful men extended beyond Phragus to the malefactor. The same word that had meant "to kill" when the thin man used it now seemed to connote banishment of a particularly benign stripe. Although the judge and the elderly man no longer addressed the thin man, as if indeed he was no longer present, they arranged housing for him beyond the old town's boundaries, where he would be able to live and breed and—Phragus foresaw in an act of blinding historical insight—produce the nation that would devour its parents.

It was more vital than ever that he communicate the nobility of the Nassyrian soul to his twentieth-century peers before the same fate that befell Eden likewise doomed the modern world. He rose to his foot and raced for the stairs, out, into the sun, to expedition central.

Mr. Salem was on the telephone to the States, detailing a Nastrokhani exhibition at the Apfelschnitt Museum, when T. A. Phragus, lame and loud, burst in on him.

"Come, quickly man. Hurry!"

"In a—"

"No!" Phragus slammed his fist down on the phone. "Now." He dragged Salem and everyone else in the office to the site. If he had stopped to ask himself what he expected them to see, the professor might have given pause, but he was too excited by his vision to delay. So, for a moment, were the students who followed him out of the last vestiges of respect for his prior renown.

Led by the limping, panting professor, the group made its way through the forgotten streets of the old town. When they arrived at the base of the temple, it was dusk, and the light seemed suspended in a layer above the stone. Phragus tramped up the three steps to the temple plateau, with Mr. Salem and his students behind him. But when they reached the spot where the staircase had been, there was no evidence of a staircase in sight.

"Rot, the trap's shut," Phragus grumbled. He rapped angrily at the stone with his crutch. "Here," he said. "You have to pick at the mortar and the hinge will swing like—Damn, we'll dig it up then."

The students' expressions showed their doubt, but dig they did because they could not deny his delirium. Mr. Salem stood with his arms crossed and the sweat trickling down his spine while Phragus paced back and forth beside the kneeling students. Finally, they lifted the heavy slab. A large, multiribbed worm, disturbed by the sudden exposure, crawled sluggishly under the adjoining square.

"I couldn't . . . I must have made a mistake. Here, this stone here," Phragus said.

This time, nobody moved.

Mild as Arthenius ordering the decapitation of Lette, Mr. Salem asked, "Would you like to tell us exactly what is on your mind, Professor?"

"I can speak the language."

"And what language might that be?"

"Nassyrian."

"Nonsense." Mr. Salem was losing his patience.

"There are men down there and they speak Nassyrian. They taught me."

"Professor, let me inform you of the facts. One: There are no 'men' down there. Two: That we can read the language at all after the detour you took us on is something of a miracle. And three: Nobody knows what it sounds like. We can't speak it."

"We have to."

"Professor . . ."

Theodore Aloysius Phragus was red as a brick with humiliation and outrage. Yet he knew that he had to overcome his personal weaknesses for the sake of the greater truth. "No, you have to understand. I understand the secret of not being. *Bename*

Nassyhalaho. I can prove it. *Yuffa lustig* the tablets. *Yuffa nestor* the symbol. *Yuffa . . .*" His English was cracking and a group of high-pitched sounds seeped out between the syllables, like water through a broken dam.

The students glided warily back, sensing the danger of his mind.

Unaware that his behavior evoked his nickname, Froggie's eyes bulged and tongue wagged.

The students stared at him as if they were deaf, and the harder he tried to explain, the more distant they looked.

He saw that they were utterly incapable of comprehension. Then someone put a tender hand on his shoulder, but he shook it off violently. Someone else stepped forward to restrain him. He jerked about, and then, with a strength born of his desperation, he used his crutch to vault a low wall and escape into the desert.

EPILOGUE FROM *The Journal of Hermeneutic Socio-Anthropology*, a review by Edward Generus of *The Wild Man of Nastrokhan* by Drs. Claude Morraine and Samuel Salem.

In this pioneering study of the degeneration of language skills, Professors Morraine and Salem break new ground from their previous archaeological researches. Treading gently in the potentially treacherous field of psychological·linguistics, they candidly acknowledge that they ventured here only because circumstances put them in possession of a unique phenomenon. The professors protest too much. Their work is a classic.

During the summer of 1983, a one-legged madman appeared on the periphery of the archaeological dig in Nastrokhan (viz., *The Kingdom Rewoven*, Claude Morraine, 1981). He was, or had once been, a Westerner, as was evident from the cut of his tattered clothes. His white linen trousers were bunched at the waist and tied with a scrap of rope. Apparently, he lived in the caves on the outskirts of the encampment, from which he would emerge to forage for food. Occasionally, the diggers would surprise him, but more often than not it was the reverse. He would appear on top of a wall, ranting down like a biblical prophet.

A point of particular interest to the authors was that the madman ranted in an imaginary language. His meaning was obvious from his tone, alternately beseeching and furious. Nonetheless, his words belonged to no known linguistic group. Professors Morraine and Salem go off on a number of eloquent tangents relating to the nature and origin of languages and the eternal debate over whether it is the man who makes the language or vice versa. They hypothesize that grammatical and syntactical variations may prevent the users of different tongues from understanding each other, because they cannot share the most basic preconceptions of being.

The madman, however interesting an opportunity for speculation his speech provided, became a nuisance when he began to write. He employed the identical symbols as the Nassyrian language for his imaginary language. This was distressing because he carved his symbols into obscure niches where they were likely to be found by the staff and mistaken for the real thing.

Finally, the professors decided to track and catch the madman, for his own good. Having made this decision, however, they were no closer to implementing it. Despite his handicap, the man was as elusive as the Loch Ness Monster. Everytime the members of the expedition thought they had him cornered, he managed to evade them through a hitherto secret passage. Some began to doubt his existence; some called him a ghost. Professor Salem ordered a round-the-clock guard for the most important excavations, but the man sneaked in and carved at will.

Then, Professor Morraine himself, who had been coordinating the hunt from New York, came to Nastrokhan. Together he and Professor Salem and a new contingent of dedicated volunteers embarked on what they had determined would be the final chase. As a trap, they built a mock excavation from which they carted boxes of fake artifacts. Sure enough, one day after dusk, the lunatic slid out of the shadows with a primitive chisel in hand, set to mar the sham discovery.

Hidden spotlights flared on. The man dropped the chisel and fled back into the shadows, but this time the professors were onto him. They pursued him across the ruins of the Nassyrian capital, through the market, in one side of the great oval amphitheater where many a bloody sacrifice had taken place. Using his splintery crutch as a second leg, the old man set a dazzling pace that his younger trackers were hard put to maintain. Several times, they thought they lost him, but each time he broke across a gap between the ancient dwellings. In retrospect, Professor Salem wrote, "It was odd. He almost seemed to be leading us on."

He led them from the vastness of the new city to the closeness of the old. There, in the twisted alleys, he might have gained his freedom yet one more time, except Professor Morraine said, "This way," and took the intrepid band toward the original temple. It was nearly dawn now, and the red lights of the rising sun caused the veins in the elaborate stonework to glow. The madman dashed across the plateau. Then, he appeared to disappear.

There was a flight of stairs into a cellar at one end of the temple. Whether the madman was running for the stairs or simply forgot them is open to conjecture, but in his eagerness to escape, he misstepped, tripped, and tumbled down to the bottom, where he lay with his neck broken.

By the time the good professors arrived, the man was dead. But surrounding him in the secret underground chamber was a hoard of tablets which he had apparently constructed from water and sand in the same painstaking fashion as the first men of Nassyria. As they had done four thousand years ago, he used a stick with a wedge-shaped tip to engrave volumes of commentary. His alphabet was Nassyrian, and so were his images, in particular the one central figure of the culture, that glorious profusion of overlapping arcs and angles, but the language was his own. Of course, it is impossible to translate.

Postscript to a Dead Language

IRA KEPLER walked onto the Temple Mount, where he set
down the econ, poli-sci, and Spanish textbooks with the Signet *Don
Quixote* from his world literature course, along with a fat loose-leaf
binder divided into subjects by transparent plastic tabs. The paper
ziggurat sprawled beneath the basketball hoop. Ira stepped carefully,
so as not to knock aside any of the pilgrims, and kneeled on the
stone plateau beside the Temple. He peered through the tiny windows into the sanctuary, and lifted a section of roof to peek into the
centermost chambers, the Holy of Holies, where the High Priest
himself was allowed to enter only on the holiest day of the year.

"Anyone home?" A voice called out across the gymnasium.

Ira looked up at the pretty girl stretched out on the bleachers
who had interrupted his woolgathering. He might have been irritated by anyone else. This, however, was Kelly Whittaker, the clarity
of whose blue eyes had not been seen in Jerusalem since Richard,
Coeur de Lion, departed in 1192, the year of his Lord. "It may be
sacrilege," Ira said, "but I can't help but wonder who cleaned the
Holy of Holies."

"What do you mean?"

"I mean that if it was totally forbidden to enter the premises, under penalty of death I think, well then, who cleaned it? Who came in on Thursdays to dust? Who was God's janitor?"

"These are the questions that will make you great, Ira. Here you've created this fabulous—"

Kelly groped for the correct word, which Ira gladly supplied, "—panorama."

"And all you're worried about is lint."

"In other words, you don't know."

"True." The blithe admission of ignorance shivered his heart. There was not an ounce of dissembling in the graceful frame which spanned three of the benches that rose from beyond the turreted wall that delineated the northwestern quadrant of the Hebrew capital.

Kelly was honest and as good as she was beautiful. The only two qualities she lacked were Jewishness and that of being Ira's girl friend. He thought of his parents and what their reaction might be if he were able to snag this blond goddess. They would gag on their pastrami and then Ira's mother would ask Kelly the price of her nose, unable to believe that it might be natural.

"Show me your Temple—please," Kelly called to him.

"I'll show you mine if you show me yours."

"Please show me your Temple, Ira." Kelly rose from the bleachers and hiked across the Judean hills molded from papier-mâché. She placed a tentative foot over the wall into a tiny courtyard where a tiny tethered donkey stood in the shade of a tiny olive tree.

"No shoes," Ira cried, although he didn't know if he said this to protect his work or to see Kelly barefoot.

The enormous model consisted of a succession of hollow cubes spread with glue and dipped in sand. Inevitably the sand rubbed off, creating a layered texture as well as a dusty passage between them, which was fine. The miniature city was meant to look as if a caravan of camels had just trooped through to offer a sacrifice at the altar.

Though familiar, Ira's panorama of Jerusalem was curiously disorienting, because certain images vital to the modern sense memory of the holy city were missing. There was no trace of the famous golden dome of the Mosque of Omar, nor was the Wailing Wall visible in all its sacred decrepitude below the Moslem shrine. The Church of the Holy Sepulchre was absent in the maze of alleys winding through the area that was to become the Christian quarter a millennium when there was such a schismatic sect as Christianity. This was neither modern nor medieval but ancient Jerusalem that Ira had fabricated, precisely as it might have been twenty-five hundred years before he and Kelly Whittaker matriculated at the University of Minnesota at St. Paul.

Although their maker was compelled to improvise the passages between the imaginary manors and hovels and shops of the Old City, to place the soldiers and merchants wherever he would, descriptions of the Holy Temple itself were provided in the Bible; these he followed to the letter. He used the same Lebanese cedar and Sudanese ebony, and even incorporated chips of precious metal into the exterior in the precise proportions if not the grandiose dimensions delineated in the ancient text.

The afternoon light slanting in through transoms over the bleachers, reflecting off the maple floorboards, cast a reddish glow onto the model that reminded Kepler of the light in Israel. He had been there two years earlier on a summer exchange program before he had gone off to college. Until that July, he had no sense of himself as a modern Jew, but his parents had urged him to join a work-tour package and ultimately bribed him with the promise of a new used car.

The first few weeks of his stay on Kibbutz Yavna were excruciating, and Ira frequently wondered if a beat-up Camaro was worth the trouble. Picking oranges at 5:00 A.M. held no romance for the disaffected youth, but the air-conditioned excursions on the "volunteer's" days off ranged from the fleshpots of Eilat to the mystical village of Safed and culminated in a trip to Jerusalem, where their group stayed long enough to see the sights of three millennia. It was, however, not the individual holy spots that impressed themselves upon Ira so much as the sense that the entire city was holy. Jerusalem made the suburbanite a Jew, and its re-creation here was an inspiration he had as the airplane he had reluctantly boarded outside of Tel Aviv circled around Manhattan. Right then, he vowed to create the God's-eye perspective of the city whose preaviation citizenry only viewed it from man's humble stature.

"It's beautiful," Kelly said. She bent, and her soft knee extended out beyond the tartan plaid skirt she wore. "I mean it really makes you feel you're there where—"

Ira turned on her. "Where what?"

"Nothing."

"Tell me."

Kelly knew her answer would disturb Ira, but she could not lie. "Where Jesus walked."

Ira smiled. Despite his revelation, he still felt a profound ambivalence toward his ostensible faith. It was not so much Judaism that inspired him as the free-floating sacramental elements of the capital. He said, "I'd rather be where Kelly walks."

"Will you take me to Jerusalem?"

"Next year," he said, making a joke that she didn't understand.

Kelly didn't hear him. She tiptoed through the metropolis, enamored of detail after tiny detail. "Is that the way they really built the steps? Oh, look, that naughty dog."

"Pissing on holy places has always been part and parcel of the Hebrew tradition," another voice declared.

Kelly turned so rapidly that she inadvertently knocked over two balsa-wood camels. Their miniature packs spilled a thimbleful of cinnamon, the scent of which suffused the district.

"Earthquake," said the interloper.

Kelly stared at the older man who was standing at the entry to the gymnasium. He was wearing a dingy white suit and carrying a suitcase from between the seams of which tufts of paper stuck out like feathers from a worn quilt.

"Hello, Professor," Ira replied with surprising equanimity, since he too had no idea how long the man had been eavesdropping.

"Hello, Kepler. How goes the great project? I couldn't help but overhear your musings about sacrilege. Perhaps you would like to consolidate those into a paper for my course. I can see the title now, 'Heresy as an Act of Faith.'"

"No, thank you, I think I'm doing enough already."

"Ah, backtalk, the heart of the Hebrew manner. From whence do you think it"—he paused, and finished with scorn—"evolved?"

"I am not speculative-minded, sir."

"Yes, it is your literalness that is so impressive," he laughed, and then stalked silently about the periphery of the city. "Very good," he said. "You are almost done."

Ira bent to set upright the camels Kelly had knocked over and corrected him, "I am done."

"No," the professor insisted, "no more so than God was done once he had set each of Adam's limbs in place. You may have laid all the bricks, but until you blow the spark of life into your structure it remains inert."

"Faith must constantly re-create itself?"

"Precisely." The professor scanned the artificial metropolis one more time with evident satisfaction, and strode out the door.

As if afraid that his spirit might be lingering, Kelly whispered, "That man gives me the creeps."

"Oh, Willy's not so bad."

Ira now leaned back against the bleachers, appreciating his city. The idea born in the airplane above New York had blossomed that first semester in Minnesota, but it had taken him two years to find an adviser with the desire to encourage his project and the clout to find him the necessary space. Since the Mount alone measured five hundred feet, and the city beyond it several thousand more, a scale of one inch to five feet required thirty feet square, minimum.

Of all the professors on campus, Wilson Hemmings was the last Ira would have expected to come to his rescue. Hemmings was known as the don of creationism. He fought Darwin on his own ground, arguing from zeal backed with biology rather than mere adherence to the text. He was the one scholar that the fundamentalists pointed to with pride, the smartest reactionary west of Washington, a cranky eminence whom Ira would never have approached in his bizarre quest. It had taken two years for Ira to exhaust the Jewish faculty and the arts faculty, all sympathetic but unable to help, before he was accosted by the famous old man in the cafeteria.

"Ira Kepler?" he asked. Hemmings stood between Ira and the glass doors that opened onto a garden patio overlooking a pond where a pair of resident swans that were the school's unofficial mascots lived. The afternoon sun directly behind him, he was a huge silhouette ablaze at the extremities.

"Yes." Ira squinted to discern the features of the one-man solar eclipse.

"I am Wilson Hemmings."

Ira noted that the man did not say, "My name is Wilson Hemmings." "I am" was a matter of equivalence, recalling God's identification of himself to Moses in the burning bush, "*Hee-nay-ni.* I am that I am."

Ira knew who he was anyway; the professor was famous and distinct. Nobody else wore a suit the same dingy color as the swans, shoulders asag from the weight of a suitcase crammed with manuscripts that he lugged everywhere.

The man that was Hemmings continued, "I hear that we share an interest."

Before Ira could suggest that this was extremely unlikely, the elderly man sat down and revealed his own sketches for a temple drawn from his own Bible study. One after another, he pulled them forth from the interior of the suitcase, architecturally impeccable, delicately colored with the hues of antiquity, but bent and soiled from being dragged around the world by their neurotic designer.

"Why?" Ira asked.

"Because the Temple must be rebuilt to usher in the Messiah. You think I'm nuts, and that's fine. You have your reasons. I have mine. We both want the same thing."

Moreover, Hemmings knew that although the old gymnasium was due for the wrecking ball, it was likely to be delayed indefinitely because of the state's fiscal crunch. If they couldn't raise funds for the new fine arts center, there was no reason to demolish the old gym. Wilson Hemmings was on the Board of Trustees that governed the university. If he requested the use of an empty building for a scatterbrained project, there wasn't a dean who would dare say no.

"Why do you need me?"

"It must be a Jewish temple, Kepler."

"To recall Jesus?"

"Forget my motivations. Willfully forget. That should be irrelevant to you." He grinned, revealing bad teeth. "Your motivations are certainly irrelevant to me."

Ira sipped the tepid brew that passed for coffee in the Student Union and agreed to build, despite the distinct sensation that he was signing his name in blood.

Now, many months later, he explained to Kelly: "God gave the people of Israel moral instruction and led them to historical action, but through the millennia he told them to build only one thing, the Holy Temple. The Bible is quite explicit on construction advice, on measurements and materials. All you have to do is follow the dotted lines and build what the divine architect tells you. You see that's the trick of the Bible, listening, remembering, not forgetting."

Two pigeons swooped under the beams, which crossed the air under a row of milky glass transoms.

"What about Noah's Ark?"

"Noah wasn't a Jew." Ira was reminded of one of Professor Hemmings's harangues as they planned their city prior to breaking ground.

The creationist had insisted on approving Ira's ideas, but the week before Christmas, he revealed some of his own rationale for the endeavor, harking back to the earliest of biblical epochs. "And God sent forth a dove to determine if any land had yet emerged from under the seas," Hemmings avowed. "To form a new, sinless universe. And what has been the result?" Hemmings asked the young man. "Sinless, indeed. Here, among the young and presumably innocent we have rampant drug abuse, fornication, abortion, pornography, rebellion. Sinless, indeed! Create a new world, Ira Kepler. Use the Bible as your guide and create a small, perfect place. And we will send forth a—" He paused and, because he was a scientist as well as a madman, spoke accurately, ". . . pigeon to determine if there is a harbor for us."

"I've got a class," Ira replied.

"What subject?"

"History."

Hemmings looked like a pigeon had gotten caught in his throat. But if the only tool to the re-creation of the Temple Mount in Minnesota was a Jewish history student, he had to swallow his fears and let it be.

Soon after, Ira was able to begin his model of the Holy Temple. The old gymnasium inhabited by the shades of Knute Rockne's generation was perfect. He assembled his materials, maps and guides tacked to the walls like blueprints, pots of glue and sixty-pound bags of sand, and a mountain of square wooden blocks from a supply house that sold them to nursery schools. He worked every evening. He neglected his schoolwork, except for history, but under the aegis of Wilson Hemmings none of his other teachers complained. He had been given tacit leave by the religion faculty, a sort of student's sabbatical. It wasn't until he was nearly done that any other distraction entered his life.

Ira met Kelly in history; they were discussing the French Revolution. She was a local girl of Huguenot heritage, who understood nearly as well as a Jew what the terrors of the past meant in the blood. One day, while Ira was mulling over his plans for a ceramic-tiled terrace, Kelly sat beside him.

"What do you major in?" she asked.

Uncertain of his vocation, Ira asked in return. "What does major mean? It sounds so military."

"What would you prefer?"

"'To emphasize' perhaps, or 'to excel.' Yes, how about the expectation that one should excel in a particular subject?"

"Right, can you imagine them," and she pointed to a group of boys in football jackets passing on the other side of the pond, "all being told to sign up for a field of excellence. Yes, I'll excel in phys. ed. I'll excel in booze and broads. What about you?"

"I'll excel in skeptical thought."

"No, really."

"If you really want to know, I'll tell you."

"I really want to know."

Ira looked at her and passed judgment upon her sincerity. A moment later, he explained what was taking shape in the abandoned gymnasium.

Kelly was thrilled when Ira described his model, but it wasn't until the following winter that she took the liberty of sneaking in to witness him laying the final blocks.

"It's perfect," she said.

"Not quite," he said. "It contains within itself the seeds of its own decay."

"Don't we all?" she asked.

"Yes," Ira said, feeling that, if anyone, Kelly would remain perfect. Together, they walked outside. The campus was cast in the white rime of an early ice storm. The wind howled, but they paused to appreciate the brittle landscape.

"Nip in the air," Kelly said with midwestern understatement.

Ira wrapped his too-thin New Yorker's coat more tightly about his midsection. "Look." He pointed toward the frozen pond between the gymnasium and the administration building.

As they watched, a stray dog placed a tentative paw on the surface, testing its solidity. The dog inched its way onto the pond, skidded, and continued toward the center, where it began gnawing at what appeared to be a large snowball.

"What's that?" Kelly said.

The dog tugged until it pulled the object off the surface of the ice and puffs of white caught in the gust. One puff wafted to Ira's outstretched arm. It was a feather.

Ira now stepped gingerly forward.

Kelly reached out.

"C'mon," he said, "let's walk on water."

They inched delicately toward the center until the cur saw them and loped away with its treasure, the head of a swan that had been frozen into place by the sudden frost. On further examination, they were able to discern the faint white shadow of the bulk of the creature beneath a tiny red circle the width of a swan's neck like a penny on the surface.

Kelly folded into Ira's jacket. He could feel the warmth of her tears on his cheeks, and they kissed silently beside the carcass of the bird.

FROM FROST to thaw was a long time coming in Minnesota, not quite as long as the period from exile to redemption, but a good four months. Ira rather enjoyed the harsh winter days in which the snow swept horizontally out of the Arctic in ready-made drifts. He was fascinated by the local radio warning of a "white out" one day when it stormed so convulsively that the horizon between earth and sky was obliterated. As protection from the wind and the whiteness, Ira finally purchased the kind of primary-color down jacket worn by all the other students, whom he called "bubble people." He and Kelly would rub a circle of hoarfrost from her window and survey the paths thousands of Timberland boots had trod into the snow.

Then one day the snow was gone and the down jackets were shed, like a swan's coverage, for T-shirts.

"It looks like California," Ira said as he observed the stream of students flowing along the trails that crisscrossed the campus on the same diagonals that had been etched into the snow. Without the landmark embankments to guide their April steps, they did not diverge an inch from their February paths, like ancient trade routes following an invisible line through the desert. These were the terms in which Ira thought as the view from the fourth floor of Centennial

Hall reminded him of his own growing city, built in from the perimeter toward the Temple.

"Every place looks like California," Kelly said.

"Except Jerusalem. Jerusalem looks like no place else on earth."

"Especially your Jerusalem," she said.

Ira lowered his head with the weight of modest pleasure this gave him. Although he thought he was nearly done the previous fall, he had persisted in refining the model city throughout the winter, adding tiny swatches of rug to the miniature bazaar and a working well with a toothpaste cap–size bucket lowered by a thread into the cistern he replenished from the water fountain, while denying that his city had attained its final state. He and Professor Hemmings had radically changed opinions in this respect, for the mentor who had once insisted upon the city's incompleteness now demanded a sign-off.

"Enough is enough," Hemmings cried in frustration at the perfectionist's delays.

"How tautological," Ira teased the senior faculty member, although he zipped his lips when Hemmings went on to rant about the sins he saw consuming the modern world with the strange unspoken assumption that Ira's city was to provide a divine rectification. Kepler, the modest master builder, disagreed, but rather than argue the point he focused on gluing the latest infinitesimal mosaic to the Temple floor, until he was left in peace for another night. There was something about his solitary moments in the cavernous gym, inserting iron brads to the top of the city gates, that was profoundly satisfying. By declaring it done, he would remove it from his own private domain. In the meanwhile, it was his and Professor Hemmings's secret.

Ira Kepler's was a life of wonderful secrets, composed and comforting as a beloved childhood quilt folded into an attic chest. There was the model which he kept from the public, and there was Kelly whom he kept from his parents. She was warm, sweet, and inspirational, but then, come the first budding of the dogwood, there was a secret he instantly knew that he had to keep from the girl he loved.

Mimeographed posters had been taped and tacked onto bulletin boards across campus announcing an "informal Haggadah" that night at the campus Hillel. It was Passover, the celebration of the Jewish Exodus from slavery in Egypt and, implicitly, the inauguration of the kingdom of God in Zion and the creation of the Temple to house the ark born across Sinai. Immersed in his own holy site, Ira had forgotten the customs of the Diaspora, but the notice drew his attention from among other advertisements for used typewriters and rides to Des Moines.

The very word "seder" evoked the holidays of Ira's youth, raucous family gatherings that partook of hand-me-down Borscht Belt anecdotes and gastronomic Judaism without the spiritual core he wordlessly sought in a room full of sand-painted wooden blocks. Nonetheless, the second he saw the green sheet with the Hebrew letters underneath the English transliteration, he knew that he would attend, strangely unfaithful to the girl who wore a delicate silver cross around her neck.

The campus was quiet as he set off from the dorm. Since it was Easter, too, most kids were on a vacation scheduled to coincide with the religious holidays that might otherwise have interfered with their diligent pursuit of wisdom and foreign beers. Kelly, in fact, had invited Ira to come with her to her parents' house. "It's only seventy miles from St. Paul to St. Cloud," she said.

"What about St. Paul in the clouds?" he had joked, but she only stared back, saddened by the betrayal she could sense approaching like a cricket a rainstorm. She had kindly offered to remain with Ira that first night of the Jewish holiday, but he lied to her by saying that he was going to work on the Armenian quarter. Kelly should have known something was wrong; in the year of his metropolis, there was no such place as Armenia.

The seder was held in a yellow-tiled basement that served the small, self-conscious Jewish community of the university. It was decorated for the festival with hanging bunches of plastic grapes and hosted by a whey-faced chaplain who tried to engage Ira in a discussion along with three religious boys his advertisement also drew. Unlike Ira, the religious boys did not need to don a yarmulke especially for the occasion, because they were never without a head covering. Like Ira, they felt at odds with campus culture, but had they known his theological trespass, they might have preferred the company at midnight mass.

"Passover is the Festival of Freedom," the chaplain announced. "Can we apply its lessons to contemporary life?" This was asked in the intentionally provocative tones of a first-year adjunct. Of course, he was met with silence.

For the religious students, the blind observance of ritual *was* freedom. They did not want to enquire into the relevance of Jewish history; if anything, they took comfort in the isolation of their faith from the world that surrounded them. Just give them a prayer book and a kosher chicken and they were happy.

Finally, Ira took pity on the chaplain by breaking the awkward pause with a question of his own: "What is Freedom?"

Only now did one of the other boys glance up from his examination of a nubby black tome. He reminded Ira of a goat in heavy black-framed glasses.

"I mean," Ira said, "just because we can say anything we want doesn't mean that we know what to say. Just because there are no bars on the doors doesn't mean that we're not prisoners in St. Cloud."

"Why did you come here then?" the chaplain asked earnestly.

Ira started to say something about the qualities of the school, lapsed into the asinine numbers he recalled from Barron's *Guide to Colleges*—the volumes in the library, seats in the stadium—and then he abruptly ceased. The truth was that he imagined the bitter cold of the Minnesota winter as ritually purifying, the antipodal equivalent to the searing desert heat of the Middle East. There was something about the temperate zone that Ira disdained. "We are here," he said, working slowly through his own thicket of concerns, "because the home of the Jews is anywhere but Israel. Or if it is Israel after all, it must be the Israel of the past, the Chosen People lost not in space but time."

"Very nice," the religious boy said.

"Unfortunately," Ira continued, "Zion is no longer within the realm of possibility. The time of miracles is over. We are ghosts in the aftermath. Our very tongue is a dead language, and everything we say is merely a postscript to a text that nobody can read."

The religious boy sneered, "A paradox."

This was not what the chaplain had in mind when he conceived his informal interlude. He suggested that the discussion had been fruitful, but that it was time they commenced the Haggadah. He was relieved that nobody disagreed.

Ira thought about the existence of his city like a pauper might think of a gold tooth in his mouth; it was all that separated him from poverty. He wanted desperately to blurt out his secret, but like the pauper reluctant to reveal his gold tooth, he did not open his mouth.

They raised four glasses of wine, enough to get Ira a bit tipsy as the chaplain read through the prayers, sang a few songs, and brought the evening to a conclusion with the age-old refrain, "Next year in Jerusalem."

MOMENTS LATER, Ira left with a feeling of profound unhappiness. As he emerged onto the hushed central quad of the
university, a familiar voice hissed his name from the bushes,
"Kepler."

"Hello?"

"There's a light on."

Ira's eyes had already gravitated toward the old gymnasium that
contained his model, so that the words were no surprise. The voice
was correct. There was a light on. He recognized the voice. "Hello,
Professor."

Wilson Hemmings stepped out from the bushes, twigs and dead
leaves adhering to the faded white collar of his suit. "How was your
seder?" he asked.

"Fine."

"You're familiar with DaVinci's *Last Supper?*"

The professor was even more elusive than usual, so Ira didn't
understand what he was getting at. "Yes?"

"It was, of course, a seder. Jesus was Jewish. The next day, the
festival of Passover became Easter. Jesus was crucified on the day of
remembrance for the liberation from Egypt. How appropriate to wait
until the current Passover to relive that upon the Temple Mount of
St. Paul."

"To relive what?"

Rather than answer, the pedagogue merely continued his lecture, "The interesting thing is that your moment of historical consciousness is enacted yearly. Not merely described, but experienced.
To the contrary, our holiday is a matter for contemplation. We celebrate it, but not in the same fashion as the Jews who say, 'I was a
slave in Mitzrayim.'"

"This is interesting, but it's late and I must say good night,
Professor."

"A pity. I thought you might wish to accompany me on this auspicious occasion. I was going to breathe life tonight."

"Into the model?"

"What else?"

Ira could not rid himself of the mechanical mindset. All that occurred to him was the raising of the hammered iron gates and the lowering of the tiny bucket into the tiny well. The lace curtains in his Temple may have fluttered with the unwanted breeze that slipped through the broken transom, but no human breath other than the city's creator's had blown upon the sacred premises. "And how were you going to go about this?"

"That is an astute question, and one well befitting the analytic Hebrew mentality." Wilson Hemmings's eyes glowed. "We will do what was done at the original. We shall reenact the day Our Lord expired."

"I'm not sure I understand."

"Think now, my little Yiddile. What is the dominant, ongoing theme of the Bible? Think of Cain and Abel. Noah's Ark. Isaac and Abraham. The Golden Calf."

Ira recalled enough of Professor Hemmings's discourse to answer correctly, "Sacrifice."

"Good," the professor beamed at the bright student.

"I still don't understand what you plan to do." Ira may have been inspired by the presence of the Temple, but he didn't know anything about its procedures. His was a static monument to the era of faith.

The professor had in mind a more active pursuit. He repeated the single word Ira had spoken in a harsh, sibilant whisper, "Sacrifice."

"I don't understand."

"The advent must be precipitated. Come in, let me show you how we shall accomplish this."

Ira was weary and wanted to get home to Kelly, but he allowed himself to be lead into the Old City he knew so well.

The Temple installation, not only the sanctuary but the workshops for its artisans and the housing for its acolytes, took up nearly a quarter of the municipality and stretched about eight feet under the basketball hoop. Kelly was lying flat, wedged awkwardly between the buildings. One arm was pressed to her side, the other stretched back and hooked around the temple itself, as if in fond nocturnal embrace. One leg was straight, the other folded underneath her. It took a moment for Ira to see the rough splinter upon which she was tied. It was a cross.

Hemmings laughed maniacally. "Not exactly a virgin birth, but a virgin is nearly as rare in this day and age."

Clearly the man was cracked, driven mad by millenarian passions.

"I, of course, shall play the Roman centurion. It is a shameful but vital role in the procedure. You will be the Jewish mob, forgive the typecasting. Now tell me, yon rabble, what shall we do to this man—just pretend it's like Mary Martin in *Peter Pan*—who dares to call himself the Child of God."

So Wilson Hemmings thought that he would be able to use this model to summon the Messianic age. That was why he had facilitated Ira's project, so that the spirit of Jesus Christ, represented in the flesh by Kelly Whittaker, would come riding into the capital of Minnesota on a white donkey.

Kelly opened her eyes.

"Your line," hissed the professor.

"You're crazy," Ira said.

"By objective criteria, yes."

"Let her go."

"Unfortunately, there are nonobjective criteria at work here. But have no fear. She must die in order to be resurrected."

Kelly looked at Ira, and this was yet more terrifying than Hemmings's dementia, for he saw in her the spirit of acquiescence. She not only wanted to be where Jesus walked—she wanted to die so that he could live. Kelly was ready to share the ecstasy of the faith that found divinity in flesh.

Now, for the first time, Ira felt Jewish as he asked himself, "What if this bizarre cosmic experiment succeeded?" He traced the forking paths of possible consequence like a true Talmudic scholar. "What if Kelly was Jesus? What if Hemmings could kill her and watch her rise?" The boy who was prepared to excel at skeptical inquiry asked himself, "What would the God of History say to that? Would the same result ensue as did the first time?" Ira wondered if this was the attitude that would lead to the Crusades, the Inquisition, and two thousand years of torment embodied by Wilson Hemmings.

In that moment, Ira understood why he had been compelled to build the city in the gym. Just as Hemmings hoped to beckon the savior of the gentiles, so Ira wished to recall the original monotheistic faith in all its initial purity.

It was Jesus's disruptive death and afterlife that ruined the sanctified remains of the early community. The spirit of Christian love, Kelly as much as Hemmings, was more deadly than hate. Jerusalem was subsequently raped, plundered, and put to the torch by the host of true believers from the Romans to Moslems, Crusaders, Ottomans, and Brits. The city wall was battered to the shape of the Jewish soul, breached and burned by each raging cultural storm as if it existed in order to be abused. How was it possible that in the endless circlings of history the Germans did not conquer Jerusalem, too?

Sacrifice, indeed, Ira thought. Forget the biblical sacrifices. Recall the historical sacrifices of the Jewish people who died with God's tacit accord, showing the same quiet toleration of their fate that Kelly revealed. Perhaps Hemmings was right. Perhaps she was the child of God, for only a divinity could be so heedless.

Hemmings persisted. "All of the . . . forces at work in antiquity have lain dormant. It is our function to wake them, set them in motion, to change and deliver the world."

Yes, indeed, and that was precisely why Jerusalem had to be rebuilt and reaffirmed as the habitation of the Jewish God. Despite Ira's temptation to allow Hemmings room enough to hang himself as well as his beautiful accomplice, the boy remained anchored in the rational Jewish tradition. He could not cede an inch to this lunatic speculation. He set to rescue Kelly on the Cross whether she deserved it or not, but first he answered Hemmings's thoughts with a succinct one-word commentary, "Bull."

"Sorry, that's Crete. Pagans. We're all deists here."

If this was the movies, Ira would have suddenly noticed a hanging set of rings, swung over the rooftops of Jerusalem, and swept Kelly to her freedom. He might have cleverly loosened a torrent from a nearby water tank to flood the holy city and ride Kelly to safety like an ark. If this was the movies there would have been no problem, but despite the villain's baroque messianic fetish, Professor Hemmings was sufficiently evolved to have possession of a revolver currently aimed straight at Ira's head. This was one argument the boy dared not contest.

"You can't."

"Don't be mundane, Kepler. You may be Jewish, but you're no idiot." Hemmings approached Kelly over the rooftops, carrying a handful of crude square-topped nails and a blunt mallet. For a moment, he put them down beside Kelly's head and examined the Temple that he was planning to sanctify with her blood.

Ira sat on the bleachers. He said, "I didn't mean that you can't enact the sacrifice. It's just that you're not allowed in the Holy of Holies, under penalty of death."

"Curiosity is a Darwinian trait."

"Don't go."

"I wasn't planning to."

"Thank God."

"Forget it," Wilson Hemmings declared. "The time for revelation is now." He reached down to pluck the tiny terra-cotta square of roof from the Temple of the Jews.

A beam of light sought the hollow and illuminated the chamber known as the "Holy of Holies." Although the High Priest was allowed into this room only once a year, on Yom Kippur, Wilson Hemmings felt free to bend over and look like an alchemist peering into the crucible. He had nothing to fear from eternal mysteries; he had God on his side.

Suddenly, the professor clutched at his chest and lurched sideways. He bumped over a series of secondary temples on the Mount. The columns of one smacked into the next, setting off a chain reaction. Blocks scattered every which way. Pilgrims and camels were buried under the ruins.

Blinded by his vision, eyes rolled up under his lids, Hemmings tripped across Kelly's outstretched legs, and collapsed over the plateau balustrade into the residential district of Jerusalem. The whole panorama shook with the impact. Tiny rugs went flying from the racks on which they had been displayed. Tiny ceramic pots spilled their grain. Tiny cups of coffee at tiny café tables splashed onto the ground. The papier-mâché foundations cracked wide and swallowed entire districts.

The devastation was universal, and Hemmings lay with his head resting on a turret knocked back into the Valley of Gehenna. It resembled a crown.

A small voice moaned, "Please, Ira." It was Kelly.

The boy knelt down to untie her bonds, but the girl remained prone and repeated her appeal, "Please, Ira." She was begging him to finish Hemmings's unfinished labor. It would have been easy, and for a moment Kepler was tempted. The mallet and nails were still awaiting their victim. Instead, he reached over the cross and reclaimed the square of roof from the grip of the man who dared to peek at what all men were forbidden.

Ira gazed across the city from his vantage point on the Mount. It was ironic that twenty centuries after the Temple itself was destroyed, the city of Jerusalem remained intact, yet here the city lay in ruins while the one structure that stood tall was the Temple. The only piece that was missing was the square that Ira held in his hands. This meant that Ira had one final task to achieve, one final truth to determine. The believer might die, but the Jew could not avert his eyes.

Prepared to reset the tiny panel onto the naked beam, he couldn't resist. Ira whispered, "Sacrifice," and peered over to see what the dead professor had seen, the image of his faith, the swastika.

Himmler's Chickens

IT WAS a three-by-five index card, worried at the edges, with thin black ink letters that shifted midcard from capital to small as the writer ran out of space for his urgent communication.

FOR SALE—MUST SELL
RARE FOOTAGE
KILLING HIS BELOVED BARNYARD PETS
as the war came to its sad conclusion
heinrich himmler
call roy 787-4221

THE NOTE then changed into script, falling off the bottom of the card, "leave no message."

The card was tacked to the bulletin board in the small glassed-in foyer to Ares: The Military Man's Bookshop, on the third floor of the commercial building at 4 Passaic Street, Passaic, New Jersey, above the L'Eleganza Beauty Shoppe and the local law firm of Kahn and Blumenfeld. The scent of hair and shampoo and a steamy mist from the improperly vented dryers of L'Eleganza rose up the stairwell and fogged the glass windows of the bookshop, obscuring the titles on display, illustrated tomes on the great battles of history from Thermopylae to Austerlitz to Antietam to D Day. General Norman Schwartzkopf's memoirs were heaped in a stack beside current and back issues of *Soldier of Fortune* magazine, next to the cash register just inside the second door. Shelves of additional volumes ran to the back of the store, protected by kit-made MIGs, Messerschmitts, B-52s, and submarines hung by fishing line from the sprinkler pipe that ran down the center of the ceiling like a spine.

More cards and scraps of paper overlapping the pocked edges of the cork advertised used cars, typing services, Civil War uniforms (with bullet as well as moth holes), and other military memorabilia. The clean white card had appeared sometime the previous week, but the owner of the establishment couldn't say when or who had placed it there. He had installed the board as a public service, and tended to winnow the ads about once a season, whenever he noticed it getting raggedy.

Kahn, of the firm on the second floor, was also the landlord, but he disdained his tenants and their customers. It was women on the first floor and furtive teenagers fighting battles in their head or older men nostalgic for the trenches on the third; war and beauty were the opposing verities, and Kahn sat in the middle, defending shop-lifters and petty crooks, doing tax and estate work and real estate closings, providing paper services for the more mundane actuali-ties of life. Originally a tenant of number 4, he had purchased the structure with egregious bad timing, months before the county courthouse announced a move to new premises on the perimeter of town.

Like Ginsberg's, the local department store, the court system abandoned Passaic's once-vibrant center to an increasingly ethnic population. So Kahn was taking a night course in immigration law to be able to assist the Poles and Dominicans who wandered upstairs, noticing the gilt on the window that meant "lawyer" for those who could not read the language. There was no advertisement for the bookstore, but those who considered war a hobby found out about it through small ads in the classified section of *Conflict Digest.*

"Fifteenth of the month," Carla, Kahn's secretary, said between clenched teeth.

Blumenfeld was in Florida more frequently than not, and that created problems between the partners, but rent was rent—it had to be collected—and Kahn made the ritual trek up the last flight of stairs, which leaned more precipitously every week, to retrieve what Eisenfrucht usually had waiting for him in a manila envelope. The man paid late, but he paid in cash.

Kahn detested the distinctive pulpish scent of Ares, but dared not complain because Eisenfrucht would blame it on L'Eleganza's damp fumes. A simmering animosity between the two tenants was ostensibly caused by the venting, but the real issue was that the frills and luxury of muliebrity scared away some of Ares would-be-macho customers while L'Eleganza's owner, Monsieur Claudio Smitalle, a.k.a. Clarence Smith, resented the upstairs neighbor who paid much less rent than his own street-level dues.

Kahn himself was frightened by the bloodthirsty atmosphere upstairs, but, leaving with the envelope with two hundred dollars tucked under his elbow, he stood, transfixed at the bulletin board.

"FOR SALE—MUST SELL . . . heinrich himmler."

Kahn was Jewish, not as his ancestors in ritual garb and ongoing faith, but as his suburban peers. His wife went to Tabatchnik's to buy bagels and lox every Sunday morning, and together they went to synagogue on Rosh Hashana. Nonetheless, he read newspapers with an eye to Jewish names, took obscure pride in Barbra Streisand's career, and peppered his conversation with words like *hondle* and *shvartz*. Suddenly, however, a world of images from his childhood swelled across the periphery of the bulletin board.

Kahn had grown up in Passaic and had gone religiously to Saturday matinees at the Roxy theater, where the double bill was divided by a newsreel. Between the latest Kirk Douglas thriller and the B film, he watched Gabriel Heatter report from Europe. "Shocking, shocking," the suave reporter intoned. "As American soldiers marched into Bergen-Belsen this week they were greeted with signs of the Hun's savagery that no man could have imagined. . . ." The newsreel at the kiddie show compelled the ten-year-old to slam his eyes shut.

In a trance, Kahn turned back into the store, past the professionally neutral eyes of the proprietor. The aisles were organized by types of warfare and historical designation. By far the largest category was World War II, which included the North African campaign, the Pacific theater, and the concentration camps. Some books were dense with text and footnotes, but more were illustrated. He bought a sampling of the latter. They were expensive. Unprepared for such an indulgence, he was compelled to dig into the manila envelope under his arm to return nearly two weeks' rent to a grinning Eisenfrucht, who wrapped the purchase and handed it over while refraining from chuckling, "Come again." But still pictures were not all that Kahn craved. On a fevered impulse at the top of the stairs, he jotted down inside the cover of *In the Depths of Darkness*, "787-4221 roy."

"Have fun?" Carla said as he entered. "You were gone long enough."

"Any calls?"

"Two. Myrna and Jack."

Myrna was Kahn's wife and Jack was his best client, a residential landlord who funneled all of his dispossess work through the firm.

He went into his inner office, which was cramped by a rolltop desk that he would have preferred to trade in for something sleek and Scandinavian. But the desk had come with the premises, and sometimes he thought that his diplomas did too, together with a studio picture of Myrna and the kids, and a certificate from the Clifton Jewish Center, which he had helped with a fund drive years ago, when the kids were enrolled at Hebrew school and the courthouse was still around the corner and you could walk after dark without a police escort. He dialed 787-4221.

"Allo?" a strong female voice answered.

"roy, please."

"Not here."

"Tell him . . ." Kahn started as if speaking to some other attorney's legal secretary, but he suddenly remembered the line at the bottom of the card that said "leave no message" and said, "I'll call back," and hung up, shaking.

Rather than call Myrna or even Jack, he leaned back and perused the volumes he had bought on a whim. Many of the images were familiar. Perhaps he had seen a few of them in the daily newspapers forty-plus years earlier, when he was the same age as the anonymous boy marched at the barrel of a machine gun along the streets of Warsaw. Of course, he was still the same age as that boy, if that boy survived, but that was different. Everything was different. Passaic was different. It had been a community that raised money for the refugees in the old shul, since shuttered, its congregation moved to the cleaner, safer single-family neighborhoods of Clifton, which surrounded the festering urban core of Passaic like a horseshoe around a pile of manure. He lived in a house built by one of the refugees, a man who was hired as a janitor by the synagogue and was the richest man in town two years later, who now lived in a Tudor mansion in Montclair.

Other photographs were new to Kahn, but all conveyed the same brutal history. Some portrayed the victims, although it was hard to see the jowly local builder in the post-liberation bag of skin and bones, and some the victimizers, and he flipped through the index. Shadowed by a column of entries for the most central "H" name, he found a substantial block of numbers for the name he was seeking. Turning to page 62, he found the photograph of a small man with round glasses that caught the glare of the sun. The man wore leather boots and a stiff visored hat that sat awkwardly on his close-cropped head. There was no mention in the entries of "barn-yard pets."

T H E   N E X T   day, Kahn stood outside 4 Passaic Street for as long as he dared, watching the men who slid along the street toward his building. By noon, he felt that he could identify Ares's customers a block away; they had a studiedly idle gait that suddenly became directed as they passed PJ's Luncheonette. It was the same walk other men used across the boulevard where the old Roxy theater now showed X-rated films. "Just passing by," they seemed to announce until they made a beeline for the entrance. When the same men came downstairs with their wrapped cache of paper blood, Kahn ran up the stairs to see if a new card had appeared, but it didn't, and he started to worry that the rare footage had already been sold. He cursed himself for not noticing it earlier, and couldn't bring himself to ask Eisenfrucht if he knew anything. When Carla left that night after a snide, "Working late?" he locked himself in and dialed roy.

This time a man answered. "Hello," he said with a slight foreign accent that was not German.

"roy?"

There was a pause.

I'm calling about the ad you placed at Ares . . . the Military Man's Bookshop."

"Five hundred dollars."

"In good condition?"

"Mint."

"And you can prove its authenticity."

"The film speaks for itself."

"May I see it, first?"

"As long as I see the money, first."

"And where shall this, um, transaction take place?"

roy gave an address in an unfamiliar section of Wallingford, the town on the opposite side of Passaic from Clifton, across the river.

"And when?" Kahn was a stickler for details.

"Say ten o'clock tonight."

"Yes, I can make it, but I need to know one more thing."

roy waited.

"What sort of barnyard pets?"

roy laughed, and began to squawk and cluck and laugh until Kahn hung up the phone.

KAHN WAS not a drinking man, but he lingered over two beers at PJ's until the day man left and an unfamiliar night man came on duty. He thought of Myrna, alone at home since the kids had gone off to college, Mark at Rutgers and Ellen at Skidmore. Kahn had lied to his wife, saying that he had a closing at another lawyer's office, and would probably be home by the network news. He nursed another beer and watched the streetlamps blink on at an irregular pace along the avenue, illuminating wrought-iron benches beside Plexiglas bus shelters. The pink-and-green neon curlicues of the Roxy's marquee grew brighter as the sky grew darker. Music began to emerge from a nearby Spanish discotheque that had once been a King Kullen supermarket. Kahn looked at the clock attached to a Pepsi advertisement over the suddenly unfamiliar counter, and ordered his fourth beer.

Life in Passaic had been comfortable once upon a time. There was a row of wool mills that provided the local men with jobs and nice shops along Passaic Avenue and a high-school basketball team that set a state record for victories in a season. There was a hospital surrounded by a district of slate-shingled doctors' homes, since transformed into boardinghouses owned by the families that had served the surgeons as maids and gardeners.

Kahn had followed the path of post–war assimilation marked out for him like cha-cha footsteps on a dance floor. His father arrived in America thirty years earlier and he lived exactly as if he was still in the Old Country, going to synagogue twice daily and working long hours as a ritual slaughterer. The one major difference between his life and the life of his own parents in the Russian Pale of Settlement lay in his expectations for his son. So the younger Kahn was the first in the family to attend college, starting at Rutgers in New Brunswick and then moving on to Rutgers Law School in Newark, which had Passaic's troubles times six. Probably the last time he and Myrna had been in Newark was for the twenty-fifth anniversary of his graduating class. The area was considered so dangerous that a shuttle bus took them from the parking lot to the reception. Now his son was in New Brunswick, and Kahn feared that the institution wasn't what it used to be, tainted by the generation that couldn't get a job because it took drugs, or vice versa.

After establishing his practice, Kahn, along with the other emigrants from Passaic, purchased a home in Clifton, where he joined the new low-slung Jewish center that had an atmosphere designed to be different from the shul in which his father worshiped, a three-story brownstone that was ultimately sold to an evangelical mission, which fed the local homeless on lentil soup and the Gospels. Kahn's only remaining tie to Passaic was the office which he bought because it was near the courthouse, and then the courthouse moved and he was left stranded with L'Eleganza and Ares.

Carla acted as if she ran the office, which, in a way, she did, and the women who came to L'Eleganza left with elaborate lacquered hairdos. Kahn used to imagine them heading for film sets improvised in a motel where they would remove all of their clothes to perform acts for the cameras that would be shipped directly to the Roxy theater.

He was tempted to go across to the Roxy, dash into the ornate lobby where glass cases used to showcase coming attractions. Who knew who might see him during the afternoons; in the night he might get away with it. Myrna had not aged well, but he was honest enough to note that he avoided confronting his own unimposing features in the mirror nowadays.

Gray where he wasn't bald, forehead lined and cheeks asag, Kahn didn't know where it had all gone wrong, but he remembered a moment of high intellectual life in college, reading *Augie March*, and he could have paraphrased its beginning, "I am an American, Passaic born . . . and go at things as I have been taught . . . first to knock, first admitted; sometimes an innocent knock, sometimes a not so innocent . . ."

"Closing time in five minutes," the night man said, after swabbing the counter in front of Kahn for the second time. It was almost ten.

THE MIDDLE-AGED lawyer drove slowly across a bridge made of perforated beams of steel that looked like an erector set, and into Wallingford, a more blue-collar, industrial town than Passaic. There was a Ford dealer and a deli, a karate school, and a laundromat, but mostly there were factory buildings set on piles over the dark waters, into which they secretly pumped their waste.

The address of his destination was a shingled house wedged between a gas station and a cinder-block warehouse. There was a pile of black garbage bags beside the curb. Kahn examined the house. It was entirely dark, and the nearest light came from the gas station, but even in the gloom he could see that the house's paint was peeling and its shutters askew. "What am I doing here?" he asked himself as he stepped out of the car, and walked, unsteady from the unaccustomed drink, up a sidewalk that had heaved during the winter.

There was a note on the door, on an index card, written in capital letters that shifted to small halfway down the series of faint blue lines: "NEXT TIME COME ALONE/yours, roy." And written in script across the bottom, "Make that $750."

INFURIATED BY the arrogance of the man, Kahn was damned if he would call again, but the next afternoon he tossed Herman Rodriguez's immigration petition across his office in disgust after failing to grasp its simple points on the third futile reading, and picked up the phone.

The man, roy, was worse than before. "I thought you'd call."

"You didn't say that I should come alone, and, besides, why should I come alone? Besides, I did come alone."

"But you didn't leave alone, Counselor."

Kahn paused until he understood. "You followed me."

roy made it explicit. "One has to know who one is doing business with, doesn't one?" And once again he broke into barnyard cackling, and Kahn could almost picture the man, phone clamped chin to shoulder while he balled his fingers into fists, wedged them into his armpits, and flapped and continued his insane chicken imitation until Kahn couldn't bear it anymore and hung up, knowing as the phone touched its cradle that he would press the redial button a moment later.

Footsteps roused him, and he dashed to the landing in time to see two leather-jacketed boys ascend the final stairs to Ares.

Carla sat at her desk and appraised her frantic employer with the same cool eye as she might a wife beater in the waiting room. "Looking for clients? The ambulance went the other way."

"I'm leaving early. Leave any messages on my desk. No, forget that. Leave no messages."

He couldn't resist cruising through Wallingford on his way home. In daylight, the house didn't seem as ominous as it had the night before, more ramshackle and pathetic. But if the house appeared normal, everyone he passed on the streets looked strange, as if the postman carrying a package was roy, and the package a letter bomb he was delivering to a prominent Jewish attorney, which might not be so bad since it might create space for less-prominent Jewish attorneys.

His mind was circling around his Jewishness as it hadn't since his Bar Mitzvah, or rather his son's Bar Mitzvah, as he left spying on roy's house, and shortly thereafter pulled his car into the asphalt expanse in front of his own split-level abode less than three miles away, in a neighborhood of saplings and cul-de-sacs, just off the highway that led to the Willowbrook Mall. Yet he carried in his pocket the $750 in cash, collected from certain clients who preferred to pay their legal fees with unmarked bills. But why, he wondered, did he covet the movie of a monster, and how did he know in his belly that it was authentic?

Myrna was surprised to see him so early.

"I had a headache."

"Do you need to see a doctor?"

Her solicitousness was touching and irritating. "No, I need to lie down. What's for dinner?"

"Chicken," she said, and he laughed.

"What's so funny?"

"It's a private joke."

Thirty years together, and he had private jokes. Myrna sulked into the kitchen, where she spread a layer of jarred apricot flavoring on the legs and thighs she then sent into the oven.

Kahn sat in an enormous recliner in front of the television, in the den decorated with his children's signs of accomplishment. There was Ellen's second-prize ribbon for horseback riding, and Mark's soccer trophies. Where were his son and daughter and what were they doing? He twisted uncomfortably in the chair, and when the dinner was placed in front of him, he pushed it away in disgust.

"Myrna?"

"Yes."

"Do you believe in God?"

Holding a half-gnawed bone poised midway to her mouth, Myrna looked at her husband, and replied, "I got my hair done today."

He blinked.

She continued, "What sort of a question is that?"

"We never talk about important things."

"We talk about the children. Mark called while you were out at that closing last night."

"We go to synagogue once a year, but we belong in the same way we do to the country club. Is this kosher?"

"Bernstein is a ripoff. It's the same bird as the supermarket sells, except his has some rabbi's name stamped on the *tuchis* and costs four dollars more. Why waste? It goes to tuition."

Did people think his father was a thief? Kahn remembered his father in a bloody smock, cleaver hung from a leather loop at his side, next to the tsitsith fringes he wore until the day he died in

Passaic General Hospital of a gunshot wound. The teenager who killed him stole three steaks, two of which he ate before he was caught and sentenced to five years in jail. Kahn was confused. He had thought he knew the dimensions of his life, but a potent force had entered on the third-floor landing in front of the bulletin board, and it called all of his assumptions into doubt. He persisted, "Do you believe in God?"

"Well, sure, why not?"

"Because all I see is mortgage applications and judgments for alimony and no one enters my office happy."

"Does God make you happy?"

"Me?"

"One. Does God make one happy? Is that His purpose?"

"Well, I guess I don't know, and I feel my uncertainty. If there isn't a God, why are we Jews?"

"The hairdresser wanted me to try a bun, but I just wanted a trim and a tint. Do you like the color?"

It was blond.

"I'm just worrying."

"You know, while I was waiting for the color to set I read this article about male menopause."

"Just because I'm asking questions does not mean that I've got one foot in the grave."

"Why not?" Myrna laughed. "I do. We can dance."

Kahn and his wife waltzed upstairs and fell upon the quilted bedspread like teenagers. Half an hour later, panting with exhaustion, and giggling, "Maybe there is a God," Kahn was appalled to hear the phone ring.

"I STILL DON'T understand why you have to meet a client at this hour," Myrna said, standing on the steps to the Kahns' neatly groomed residence. She looked fetching in a plaid flannel bathrobe haphazardly thrown over her abundant nakedness.

Kahn already had the car keys out, but his hand quivered after his quick conversation with roy, who informed him that this was the one time he would have a chance and that the price was now one thousand dollars. The keys rattled as he told Myrna as much of the truth as he could comprehend. "It has to do with God."

"Edgar!" she gasped.

"I have to go now." He stepped toward the vehicle, slid behind the wheel, and looked back toward his wife. He couldn't tell if she was speaking over the sound of the ignition or merely mouthing the words, "Be careful." Alone in his steel-and-glass bubble, he mouthed back, "I will."

The streets that Kahn traversed daily from Clifton to Passaic were cut by shadows cast by streetlights at this hour. Whenever he and Myrna went out to the movies or dinner they headed in the opposite direction toward the cleaner, farther suburbs. The brick mill buildings that hung over the Passaic River were empty of everything but the ghosts of long-gone seamstresses.

He crossed the rickety Passaic/Wallingford bridge, and almost immediately saw the lights of the gas station, and more disconcertingly, those of the house he had seen twice before. At a distance, he could tell that there was no index card tacked to the door. He carried one thousand dollars in fifty-dollar bills tucked into the sock against his clammy right calf. He felt the bills bulge conspicuously under the cuffs of the pants he had swiftly donned back at the house, but knew this was irrational.

The whole pursuit was irrational. His peers at the Jewish center, coaching Little League, eating shrimp lo mein at Mr. Choy's on Route 4 in Paramus, did not scan bulletin boards that were a fountain of pathology, let alone drink the poisoned waters. No good will come of this, he told himself. Nonetheless, he pulled beside the curb, scaring a large gray water rat from the remaining garbage bags, and turned the engine off. He stepped out of the car, walked up to the door, and knocked.

A large woman wearing a kerchief opened the door. "Allo," she said, in the same voice that had answered the telephone the first time Kahn had called, when he left no message.

"Hello, is roy here?"

"He is waiting . . ." She stepped beside the door with a gesture of solemn welcome, extended a large hand with a crescent-shaped red scar across the palm, and finished the sentence, ". . . in the Jewish room."

The entry to the Jewish room was evident on the far side of a sparsely furnished salon, through an arch, perhaps created for the purpose, spanned by a wrought-iron model of the sign that also greeted the guests at Auschwitz, *Arbeit Macht Frei,* "Work Makes One Free."

Kahn was not a scholar of the war. He remembered the horrific images of his youth and had recently spent hours reacquainting himself with those images in the books he had purchased at Ares. He had ignored his own work and been compelled to ask for an adjournment of several cases before the local criminal courts. Carla had pointedly let his unanswered stack of correspondence build up on the corner of her desk.

The room itself was a small library and museum, its wall space covered by bookcases and framed photographs of German leaders, its floor crowded with display cases containing yellow stars, iron crosses, a twisted tangle of barbed wire, documents, maps, diagrams, and in one, a tiny scale model of a lager with intricate miniature barracks and a set of train tracks that reminded Kahn of the Lionel set he had installed in the basement when Mark was eight years old.

The tracks led to a tiny red brick building from which a pencil-shaped chimney rose and emerged through a tiny hole cut in the display glass to accommodate the exhaust.

While Kahn stared at the exhibit, a train, its sides encased in tiny wooden slats, emerged from a tunnel underneath the case. It chugged between the barracks and stopped at the small brick structure. Several tiny men and a tiny dog came out of the structure to meet the train, and the heavy wooden doors of the train slid open. All of the figures were rigid, but they moved with a kind of grace on their own tracks, set beneath the surface of the exhibit and nearly invisible in the dim room. Now a cluster of additional figures appeared at the door of the car, tiny naked men and women and a few even tinier children, who paused and then slid along their own tracks which led between the men and the dog, into the brick house.

Kahn looked around the room, but couldn't see where the controls were or who was directing them. Whoever it was must have switched on a tape recorder, because a slight shrill wailing was suddenly audible, coming from inside the display case. Underneath the cries of pain, he could just barely make out the sounds of Jewish prayer, "Sh'ma Yisroael."

The show was nearly over. There was one final effect. The sounds of humanity gradually faded to silence and then a thin plume of smoke arose from the chimney and Kahn jumped back.

"Welcome," roy said. "It is so good to meet another aficionado." The last word rang strangely in his blunt vocabulary, but he was obviously pleased by its use.

roy was a narrowly built, elderly man with awkward shoulders. Perhaps he was a retired mail carrier, his body distorted by decades of hauling a mailbag slung over the right side of his body. He had thin gray hair that he combed across his scalp to cover a bald spot, and he wore a vest and matching pants over sneakers.

"The film?" Kahn croaked.

"The money?" roy answered.

"Yes, I have it right here." Kahn started to reach down.

"Never mind, I trust you," roy said.

Kahn, kneeling, looked up, astonished.

"In your shoes, or socks. That's where people always carry money. There or hidden in the lining of their coats. That's where one looks. You should be more inventive."

Kahn retied shoelaces that didn't require retying.

"Be seated, please." roy gestured toward the one chair in the room with the same motion as the woman who had opened the front door. The chair was a formal wing chair, half-hidden by the drapes over the one window in the room. It sat next to a small table on top of which sat a movie projector, its front angled upward upon a book.

roy stood at the opposite end of the room and pulled a screen down in front of a framed poster urging the citizens of Hamburg to vote in the 1933 Reichstag elections. Then he walked back and stood on the opposite side of the projector, holding a gray metal cannister he had removed from a yellow cigar box filled with similar items. "I am sure that you will enjoy this," he said as he painstakingly threaded the half-inch strip of amber celluloid into the machine.

Kahn felt nauseous and wished to flee, but he couldn't leave the chair. His fingers gripped each arm as rigidly as a condemned prisoner clutches the arms of an electric chair. The lights went off.

Then roy flicked on the projector. It made a soft buzzing noise and cast a white square onto the screen, perfectly centered. There were burned spots at the edges.

A farm. A barn. An incongruous Pennsylvania Dutch hex sign over the bay. Picket fences. A tall man in uniform walks into the frame, as if emerged from one of the display cases in the Jewish room in Wallingford, New Jersey. He waves and smiles. His image turns blurry and then a huge silhouette of a hand reaches in front of the lens and swivels left and right and the image is clear again.

"That happens," roy apologized.

Another man enters the frame from the other side of the room. A man that Kahn recognizes, shorter than his companion, wearing round glasses that do not reflect the sun. The day must have been overcast. He glances at his wrist and senses that time is running out. He looks worried. He and the first man walk toward the barn and the camera follows, bouncing with the walk of the cameraman, going in and out of focus.

"They were difficult circumstances and the technology was not as advanced as our own," roy explained, but Kahn was beyond listening. He was there in the picture beside the two men.

They gradually approach a sectioned-off corner of the yard, where three chickens live. Two are sitting, one pacing back and forth, as worried as her master.

Kahn looked up at roy and expected sound effects, but the only sound was that of the film passing from reel to reel.

Sorrowfully, the shorter man with the glasses extends his hand. The other man reaches into a holster and gives him a gun. He bends down, tickles one of the sitting chickens under its crop, places the gun to its head and pulls the trigger. The other chickens leap up and run from their perches, one of them leaving an egg.

"This part was difficult," roy said.

The short man starts to chase the remaining chickens around the small area. He aims the gun and fires, but misses, and a fence post splinters. He aims again and the second chicken's leg disappears. The creature flops into the dirt and thrashes about, trying to rise. The man reaches down now and shoots the second chicken in the neck and it lies still. There are stains in the earth.

Kahn closed his eyes and didn't open them until he assumed the last chicken was disposed of, surprised that he couldn't hear the gun shots or the last frantic squawking on what he knew must be a silent film. He opened his eyes, too soon.

The short man returns the gun to the tall man and wipes his brow with a handkerchief he removes from the inner pocket of his jacket. He then reaches down and wipes off his boots and throws the handkerchief to the ground. He starts off the screen, but turns around, bends down, and picks up the egg.

The last of the film careened through the twin glass plates in front of the bulb and there was a white screen.

roy turned on the light. During the filming he must have donned glasses of his own, small round lenses mounted on a thin gold frame.

''TEA?'' THE large woman asked from the farther doorway, bearing a tray with a kettle and two glass cups and ornamental Tyrolean ceramicware containing milk and sugar. Wedges of lemon sat upon a saucer in case either of the men was inclined to a more bitter brew.

Kahn nodded his head slowly. He couldn't have said how he managed to disattach his fingers from their grip on the arms of the chair, but a moment later they were clasping the hot glass. He hadn't known he was shivering and gulped gratefully at the hot liquid.

"A rare artifact, you can tell," roy said once the woman left the room. He sipped at his own cup and set it down on the display case containing the miniature lager which might have been the scene of the filming. "Perhaps you are curious as to how I obtained it."

"No," Kahn found the strength to answer. "I am not curious. I don't care. Here is the money."

roy ignored the pile of damp bills Kahn retrieved from behind the acrylic support hose that were supposed to keep his incipient varicose veins from swelling. "I was working for the American army, behind the lines, as a spy."

Kahn recalled a section of Ares with a placard that read, "Covert Activity." There was a complete edition of the James Bond books, a biography of Mata Hari, and various histories of M-5, OSS, KGB, and the Israeli Mosad. Many of the same titles were visible on the large bookshelf between posters of smiling Aryan youth against a mountainous Alpine background.

"I was a mailman," roy said, and Kahn was shocked to find his initial intuition affirmed. "It gave me access to certain papers that the Allies needed. I was paid very well, but I was betrayed."

Despite himself, Kahn was interested. He croaked, "By . . . ?"

"Lizabetta, my wife, a patriot."

Kahn thought of Myrna, and wondered if she was sleeping.

"After the war—you see I did survive, despite minor disabilities incurred under questioning that keep me from siring children—I was issued a visa and allowed to settle here. I was even helped to get appropriate government employment in my chosen field, but not to the extent that I was promised. I have a small pension, meager savings, and my collection, but I require money for an operation that my wife needs."

"More tea?" the woman asked.

"No, thank you, Lizabetta."

Kahn looked at the woman and could not imagine what sort of operation she required, but he knew that Myrna had troubles too. Doctors were costly.

"Yet I must be certain that my archives go to the correct person."

Kahn was not a brilliant lawyer, but he served his clients as well as possible, and his mind had been trained to pick up pertinent details. "And I," he declared, as certain of his statement as he was when he made a petition before a municipal judge, "am of the correct faith."

"If you have faith, Counselor."

Kahn thought of Sunday-morning bagels and his name calligraphied onto one leaf of the tree of life in the fluorescent lobby of the Jewish center where he never did feel at ease. He thought of his son's Presbyterian girl friend. He thought of his intentions to visit Israel, put off time and again because of the cost and an unacknowledged reluctance to share anything with the Orthodox Jews who were bound to be on the flight, and the fear of and identification with the faces in the newsreels of his youth, and the envy he felt for the refugee who built his comfortable home. He looked slowly around the museum, and returned to roy, now tucking the three-inch roll of film into the gray metal cannister. "I've never met God," Kahn said, slowly finding his thoughts as he continued, "but the Devil sits beside Him. The Devil has a face."

"Yes?"

"We cannot see the far side of the moon or the back of a mirror, but we know that it exists."

"Yes," roy agreed. "I delivered the mail. I copied the train schedules, and I delivered them, both the original and the copy. I don't know what happened to the copy, but the original was read. And the trains ran. I never saw the far side of the moon either." He picked up the pile of money and counted it and handed the film to Kahn.

Kahn dropped the cannister into his pocket.

"Please show the gentleman out, Lizabetta."

The large woman accompanied Kahn to the door and stood there until he got into his car and drove away.

The Jew drove past the gas station and the abandoned wool mills onto the rattling metal bridge. He stopped midway, leaned awkwardly across the empty passenger seat to roll open the window, to breathe the rank industrial sewage. Then he removed the film from his pocket and flung it into the river.

The Library of Moloch

THREE HUNDRED faces stared, blinked, squinted, and otherwise engaged the camera while recounting the most awful moments of the century.

"Smoke, that is the first thing I remember, that and the body of my little sister."

"Yes, they hung the village elders by their beards."

"Oh, the experiments. I had forgotten. Of course, the experiments. What was it you wanted to know? What was it *they* wanted to know?"

The library was a four-room suite of offices in the base of a gothic dormitory in which aspiring lawyers lived, ignorant of the stories that the folks with branded arms told underneath them.

One room of the suite contained a receptionist's desk, a couch, and coffee table where academic journals gathered dust. The second room was a dustless repository of videotape disks set upon rows of sleek metal shelving, along with two monitors for viewing them. Never had both monitors been used at the same time, but the initial grants to establish the library were generous.

Then there was the director's office, and the testimony room where they actually produced the videotapes. This room had the air of a dental chamber where the patient reclined in a large padded chair, the videotape machine directed at the face like an X-ray tube, aiming to penetrate the skin to the soul. There was always a cool young technician fiddling with the dials on an imposing black console with blinking red lights and fluctuating meters. These interns from the university's School of Communication Arts were more interested in the quality of sound reproduction than the meanings of the sounds reproduced. Attending the meaning, however, was a doctor, whose gentle probing elicited the words, although here it was a doctor of letters who conducted the procedure. Delicate as he was, there was also the occasional wince and cry of pain.

Other libraries have taken lesser tasks upon themselves, to contain and construe the physical properties of nature or the intellectual produce of man. The Library of Moloch sought no less than a moral explication of the universe.

Fortunately, it had excellent source material. All that remains from the Crusades, for example, are a few moldy documents. Likewise, the other episodes of vast and imponderable iniquity, the Reign of Terror or the Conquest of Mexico, have faded from human memory, and hence perished in all but legend. There may be articles about Tamerlane or Gilles de Rais in the yellowing journals on the coffee table, but their ravages no longer have the pulse of life. The contemporary library has one invaluable resource that researchers into the more distant past do not, the victims. That was its avowed purpose, to find the victims of Moloch, to record them, to preserve their suffering, to remit immortality in return for the chronicle of their woe.

They had three hundred faces on file, nearly a thousand hours, tens of thousands of deaths described in ferocious detail. The library was a mausoleum; its librarians gravediggers. As for the individuals whose lives and memories were condensed onto half-inch tape, wound onto spools, stacked onto shelves—the hell with them.

DR. ARTHUR Ricardo, English born, American bred, headed the project. He was a highly civilized gentleman, with many diverse interests. He enjoyed chamber music, Oriental rugs, and nineteenth-century economic theory. The latter was a family hobby, because he was a nonlineal descendant of David Ricardo, the eminent mercantile essayist and apostate. In addition to his rarified pursuits, Dr. Ricardo was an avid moviegoer who regaled his intellectual friends with tawdry tales of Hollywood excess. How he found his life's calling in the Library of Moloch is a tale in itself. His specialty was medieval literature, but he realized that his students were more interested in iron maidens and auto-da-fés than they were the quest for the grail. Only if the grail was hidden within an iron maiden had they any chance of finding it.

At the moment when he was wrestling with his charges' gruesome misreadings of Ariosto, there was a scandal at his institution, the academy that housed the library. An elderly professor who was respected by all in his field (thermodynamics) was determined to have been a wartime collaborator. Nobody accused him of any personal wrongdoing, but he had signed a loyalty oath and he withheld knowledge of this when he sought to enter America. Clearly the man needed to be punished. Equally clearly, he had lived an honorable life since his youthful indiscretions. He was, in fact, a leader of the physicians for nuclear responsibility movement. Ricardo's sympathies were with the professor, but a squat little man appeared unbidden at the provost's inquiry. He demanded to be heard. "I worked at the mountain," he said, meaning the underground silos where the rockets the venerable professor had designed fifty years ago were produced, where scientists labored in isolation while slaves died to prove the learned men's theories.

Ricardo was not present when the man spoke, but a video recording of the speech circulated, at first covertly and then, by mass demand, at public screenings. The tape exerted a bizarre fascination. The professor was hounded into retirement.

"Imagine," Ricardo said to his class, "what we could do with the personal testimonies of the prisoners of the Inquisition, what that would tell us about the nature of faith in that era."

But one student said, "Can't we extrapolate backward from this witness? Does human nature change?"

At first, Ricardo wanted to dismiss the query. The first tenet of his life was progress, implying the perfectability of man. But the question bothered him. He had to admit that if human nature did change, it most certainly did so for the worse to just the degree that his generation's atrocities superseded those of the Middle Ages. Compared to the artifacts of the twentieth century, iron maidens were couture and racks no more than chiropractic devices. The stories of that one man who "worked at the mountain" were sufficient proof.

And there were many more stories. The man who gave evidence was the tip of the iceberg. There were others who worked the mines and others who stoked the fires. Who knew how many of these refugees from the land of brimstone were walking the streets, and each time one clutched his heart and collapsed to the pavement another storehouse of history died with him. Ricardo spoke to the videotaper, and together they conceived of the library. The university was eager to balance the scales of public opinion that had been tipped by the scandal. A board of prestigious names lined up to support the project. Grants were expedited, space allocated. Funding flowed.

Ricardo placed advertisements in ethnic newspapers, and contacted organizations that aided survivors. They tended to stick together. It was difficult to overcome their distrust of strangers at first, but their very cohesiveness made further testimonies easier. One by one, the men and women who lived through the war came to him. And he listened.

"Fire, a column of fire into the sky. It was night. The column must have been a hundred feet high. Maybe two hundred. I don't know. I'm no Galileo."

"Food, the lack of food. Hunger so great we would eat anything, grass, poison ivy, we would suck the juices from pieces of wormy wood. And you know what, Junior's cheesecake never tasted so good."

"The diseases, the scabs, the sores. We used to urinate on our wounds to anesthetize them. No, that's the wrong word. Anesthesia is what you do to the brain. My nephew's an anesthesiologist in Boston. Antibiotic? Antihistamine? Anti-something."

The more he heard, the more Ricardo needed. He grew insatiable. As the killers were driven to kill more and more, he wished to hear more and more of those they had been unable to kill. There were fifty thousand some of them, many more if one included those who hid in the woods, escaped eastward, or merely toiled away the war years in the brutal and often deadly labor camps scattered throughout the continent. Oh, he would tape them too, but it was the fifty thousand who had inhabited the capitols of death that he hunted, begged, cajoled, and, if necessary, bribed into telling their stories. He was like a collector who must attain not merely one of each species, but each and every one of the particular species he collects. To miss just one would mean an elemental loss.

"We arrived, and these men were beating us as soon as we arrived. With bayonets or gun barrels, screaming *Heraus! Heraus!* That means 'Move quickly!' There were dogs, tearing at people, and everyone was filing past this desk and most everyone was going to the left except for a few big guys who were going to the right. So I shouted, 'Healthy. Twenty. Carpenter,' and I started to the right. I was puny, sixteen, and a student, but I started to the right, and a soldier knocked me down. I got up, and started that way again, and he knocked me down again. Well, I got up and started that way again, and the soldier started after me when the officer in charge said, 'Let him be. He'll die anyway.'' The man looked into the camera and snorted, "Hah!"

It was interesting, despite their experience they were optimistic. Or was it because of their past that they were optimists, because they were able to conquer adversity, because ultimately they had triumphed. They had homes now, and businesses and children, and were able to follow the course of their lives like ordinary human beings, yet those who listened to them were devastated and came to believe in the inevitable doom of a species capable of such enormity.

Dr. Ricardo in particular suffered since his work at the library commenced. Yet the more he suffered, the greater his passion for his self-appointed mission. He ignored his students as he expanded his collection. One hundred, two hundred, three hundred tapes on the wall, a thousand hours of horror, and he knew them all by heart. His wife was eager to have children, but he would not breed. The tapes were his children.

Ricardo's eyes widened at the stories of misery, at the rivers of blood which ran from the tongues of the witnesses, at the mountains of ashes heaped up beneath the videotape camera, mountains to obscure the eye of the camera, to bury the Library of Moloch.

MOST WITNESSES told their stories voluntarily. These stories were equivalent to their souls yet they were willing to donate them to the Library of Moloch because they believed that to tell was to verify a past that had become dreamlike even to themselves. And after all, they were people of the book. Of course, the form was strange, but they had faith that this "tape" was a newfangled kind of a book, and they were willing to move with the times.

Yet some were suspicious. They had been convinced to go to the library by their children or coaxed by Dr. Ricardo, who had obtained their home phone numbers.

One old lady arrived wearing a large rhinestone brooch on a highly textured brocade dress. Her hair was cut short in a golden helmet. She could have been a dentist's receptionist, or a dentist's mother. When the tape started to roll, and Ricardo began by asking her to tell him "a little about yourself," she said, "Pardon me, but why do you wish to know?"

"Isn't that self-explanatory?"

"I never did understand the obvious. It usually hurt too much."

Ricardo was taken aback; he was forced to define the library's purpose. "To prevent such a thing from ever happening again."

"Ah, so you believe that my warning will keep armies from crossing borders, railroads from chugging down the tracks, fires from burning. I was not aware that I had such power."

"Well, not just your warning."

"Everybody's. Mine and Max Adelstein's and Dora Schwartz's. Poor Dora. What a responsibility. And her with pleurisy."

"Well, don't you think it is important"—and he called up a phrase from the survivors' own organizations, a deliberate redundancy that struck them as biblical in its admonition—"to remember. Never to forget."

"Ah," she nodded understandingly. "Never to forget, you say. To remember, you say. Did you ever think that we might prefer to forget?"

"But as a survivor, you have an obligation to—"

"You know, I never liked the word, 'survivor,' it suggests too much personal ability. There was no ability. There was luck. We are not survivors, but merely remainders, or the remains. And you are jackals, feasting on the last tasty flesh that sticks to our bones. Tell me, is it good?"

"That is terribly unfair. I am sympathetic."

"Leeches. Vampires. You cannot get more blood from our loved ones, so you're sinking your teeth into us. I do not think you are unsympathetic. I think you are jealous, Herr Doktor Professor."

Ricardo said, "I wish you would not call me that," his clipped words emphasizing the last of the British accent he had shed as a child.

"And what charmed world do you inhabit where wishes are granted, Herr Doktor Professor?"

"Enough! I will not be insulted. If you insist, we will stop this session."

"Oh, so you will judge the validity of my story on whether I have the proper respect for you, Herr Doktor Professor?" The tiny lady squirmed delicately in her comfortable chair, her grandmother's eyes gleaming as she removed her glasses and rubbed them on her sleeve.

Ricardo surrendered. "You are right. We cannot judge. We are not here to judge."

The old lady made a gesture, a hand floating horizontally across an empty channel. It was the rod of the shepherd who winnows his flock by determining which pass beneath it and which do not. In the Yom Kippur prayer, the U-nisaneh Tokef, that image is a symbol of God's judgment for the upcoming year, who shall live and who shall die. It was also used as a deliberate parody in the land of evil, only instead of a gnarled shepherd's rod, a sleek leather riding crop was used, and the little ones, too little to reach that glistening leather while standing on their toes so as to make their topmost curls quiver, never had the chance to be whipped with it. Their slaughter was immediate.

"So, what occurred after you were deported?"

She answered this and the other questions he posed with brisk efficiency. But then, after she described the American soldier who "liberated" the eighty pounds that were left of her, she said, "And where were you during the war, Herr Dok—"

"I was young."

"So was I," she said. "I was young and in love and in Europe."

"Bala Cynwyd."

"What?"

"It's a suburb of Philadelphia."

"A suburb. Of Philadelphia." Her voice was so skeptically in-flected that she might as well have said, "A cathedral. In Vatican City."

He bowed his head. "They call it the Main Line."

"How nice."

Her tone angered him. "It was. It was very nice. And I feel fortunate, but I do not feel ashamed. All right?"

"Fine by me." She lifted both her palms.

He said, "I don't have a gun."

"You don't need one. You have a camera."

"And what is that supposed to mean?"

"Nothing. Ignore me."

He wished he could. He had gotten what he wanted, another tape on the shelf, another cache of horror. The interview was over, but he could not leave it alone. "Jealous of what? Jealous of suffering? Jealous of death?" He tried to imitate the scornful laugh of one of his previous subjects. "Hah."

For the first time, Ricardo entered onto the record as more than an interlocutor from behind the camera, and the operator looked at the old lady as if for instruction or authorization to swivel the camera to view the professor's distress. She merely gazed into the lens with complete equanimity. Then she said, "There are two separate, inviolate realms. One is memory."

Ricardo answered as if in a trance, "And the other?"

She didn't answer, and it drove the doctor crazy. What was it that she wasn't telling him? What was it that none of them had told him? What was missing from his library? He mentally reviewed the names on the shelves. They were arranged alphabetically although they were also cross-categorized by age, sex, the nature of the torture endured, and the kind of response—from sorrow to anger to hatred to mystical contemplativeness. Yet something was missing.

And then it struck him. What bound and limited the library was that all of its subjects were victims. Where were their victimizers?

Amidst all of the workings of the man-made Hades, its transportation and extermination systems, recounted in detail for the librarians who spurred the informants to unearth even the tiniest additional tidbit concerning the kingdom of darkness, there was plenty about, but nothing from the lords of the infernal regions.

Of course, there was the legitimate desire to deny these men or their female counterparts credence. We do not want to hear their stories; we may find out how similar to ourselves they are. Besides which, the evildoers were hardly forthcoming. Though they pursued their crimes with vigor and pleasure, they were nonetheless aware that their actions were heinous. One arch-villain even said that theirs was an episode which would remain hidden. But he was wrong. The library was intent on proving that. Maybe society had failed the victims. And politicians had failed them. The clergy had failed them. But the librarians would not.

Dr. Ricardo was sure that his register of martyrs hallowed them, and that his recordings of their lives saved them. Unfortunately, the beneficiary of his largesse was not convinced. The old lady not only refused to recognize his charity, she dared to question his role. "Watch out," she said. "There is only one sentence for those who tamper with forbidden mysteries."

"Do not threaten me."

"That's not a threat. It's a prophecy."

"Well, like it or not, we are in the archival era. This library does not exist in order to examine experience. Here experience exists in order to be examined."

The old lady stood as he ranted, and tottered away on the heels that brought her height to five feet shy, but the man who held the technological rod that measured her value in the new world did not notice.

WHEN HE was finished, Dr. Ricardo was alone with his roomful of gray cylinders. The camera was off, and the lady was gone. He sat in her chair, still warm, and stared at the empty lens of the videotape machine. Looking down, he noticed that the arm of the chair had been scratched clear through to the stuffing, a mixture of straw and compressed fibers. Obviously one of the interviewees had been so tormented, his or her fingernails punctured the supple leather surface.

The library had money enough to repair the damage or replace the chair. But Dr. Ricardo was curious whose memories evoked such a reaction. He supposed he would never know. The cameras focused on the subjects' faces while he focused on the words.

He reached into his breast pocket and removed the pack of cigarettes he had purchased earlier in the day. He had smoked for years, stopped for years, and recommenced when he started his series of interviews.

"The fences were electrified. This was a blessing. One could always kill oneself when the pain grew too tremendous. Many people availed themselves of the facility."

Dr. Ricardo lit a cigarette and inhaled. The very process was soporific. So he fell asleep, and twisted in the soft contours of the chair, his head filled with images of his parents' home in Bala Cynwyd, outside of Philadelphia, ringed with barbed wire, on fire. Ashes from his cigarette dropped to the exposed stuffing.

Soon Dr. Ricardo wore a crown of flames, yet still he slept.

The flames spread. They rode across the seam of the carpeting on the floor and caught at the papers on his desk.

The fire passed into the storage room, and climbed the shelves. There the cylinders buckled under the heat, and they popped open, the tapes writhing like snakes in a burning cave, and the words of the witnesses escaped, and the pictures created by their words escaped. The guard towers, the barbed wire, the fires blackening the sky, escaped into the air along with the smoke.

Throughout the dormitory, the young law students woke with shrieks of terror. Their dreams were tainted; their beds turned to pyres. They staggered outside in their pajamas, clutching their seared case books.

Finally, Dr. Ricardo also woke, coughing up burned gray phlegm, sputtering. His precious tapes, the wall of evil that he wished to preserve, was being consumed before his eyes. He tamped out what he could, but he could not extinguish the blaze.

The librarian might have been able to save himself, but there was one more question he had yet to ask. He grabbed at the last tape on the shelf, the one that served as a bookend because the secretary had not had time to file it. His fingers blistered from the touch, but he jammed the cassette into the monitor whose cord was a glowing copper filament. Nevertheless, the machine worked.

The lady appeared on television against a background of flames. "Pardon me," she said, "but why do you wish to know?"

He punched the device's fast-forward mechanism. There was a blur, and when he lifted his finger, the lady seemed to smile as she said, "I do not think you are unsympathetic. I think you are jealous, Herr Dok—"

He hit the button again, and left his finger there for what seemed like an eternity. He lifted it to see her silence and hear his own voice from off-screen, "Jealous of what? Jealous of suffering? Jealous of death?" But where he expected to hear himself give a last, resounding, "Hah!" there was only continued silence. The machine may have been damaged by the flames, which rose up the curtains. He could hear sirens.

Suddenly the lady answered, "Yes, jealous."

"What?"

"Jealous of the Holocaust."

In his delirium, he wondered if fire was the fate of all libraries. First there was the Library of Alexandria with the wisdom of the ancient world, and now, the Library of Moloch containing what its keeper truly believed was the wisdom of the modern world. Perhaps, he thought crazily amid the mounting flames, this fate was not inappropriate, for Moloch was the fire god to whom children were routinely sacrificed. Moloch, the Lord of Gehenna, lived outside of Jerusalem in what was truly the valley of the damned, forever exiled in sight of the heavenly city.

He started to answer the flickering screen, but she would not allow him an opening.

"Jealous of having a reason to hate. Jealous of tragedy, because your life is no Charleston. Jealous of a people who refuse to submit to the impurities that surround them. Jealous of those who adhere to a broken covenant. Jealous of the sacred. So here you have it, Herr Doktor, so enjoy!"

"I do not understand."

"My poor professor. You know, the killers never understood us either. 'How,' they asked themselves, 'can these people meet our eyes? How can they persevere no matter the punishment we inflict?' Mind you, they were sophisticated; they knew that it was not merely the scourging of the body of the community, but the anguish of being compelled to acknowledge that animals like them shared the same cruel flesh we did, breathed the same vile air. But that was the part that made it easy. We knew we were looking at God."

"How could you tell?"

"Because God is made in the image of man. We met Him a long time ago, in Spain and Rome and Egypt, and more genteel spots. We saw Him in a topcoat and derby ducking into Whitehall. And we saw Him in Washington, too. The truth is, He is everywhere, but only we can recognize Him, because we are old friends. We know His story."

"Can . . ."

"Of course I can introduce Him to you. And now, my good fellow, prepare to meet your maker, for those who enter the Holy of Holies are condemned to burn. I told you. I told you, there are two inviolate realms."

That was it, that was what he had turned the videotape on in order to hear. That was the lesson for which he risked his own immolation in order to learn. "What are they?" he screamed at the tape, as the flames kissed his feet, and cracked his knees that were as immovable as if they were lashed to a stake.

Although the screen itself had begun to melt with the intensity of the heat, the image was calm. "I told you. One is memory."

"And the other—the other, please! The other!"

The lady answered, "Theology."